12/21

This book should be returned/renewed by the
latest date shown above. Overdue items incur
charges which prevent self-service renewals.
Please contact the library.

Wandsworth Libraries
24 hour Renewal Hotline
01159 293388
www.wandsworth.gov.uk

Wandsworth

Mely Quan

9030 00007 6778 2

This novel is dedicated to my family who gave me the grace and patience when I needed it the most. The outpour of support and loyalty as I spent sleepless nights writing was immense and a true show of compassion. This story has given me the freedom to express my love and creativity for romance and the supernatural, with a little erotica thrown onto the helm.

I would like to thank you for taking the time to read Petal and future books in the series. Your allegiance is greatly cherished and I hope you enjoy the magical ride on which you are about to embark!

LONDON BOROUGH OF WANDSWORTH	
9030 00007 6778 2	
Askews & Holts	
AF	
	WW21010903

Origin

I was exhausted, running across campus in the dead of night. I had to make it to the road where I could see lights and cars driving by. I kept looking behind me with painful tunnel vision. I stumbled and watched my blood drip down my hands as I held my back. My sight became dull and my breathing labored. I couldn't run anymore, my legs were giving in, struck with the feeling of painful needles all down my calves. I cried as I fell to my knees and put my head down. Those bodies, what human could do such a thing to innocent lives? Their blood was draining out of them, their faces imprinted in my mind. I laid on the cold wet pavement, my shirt torn, my pants ripped to shreds, and rain camouflaging my tears. Hitting me like a million tiny icicles, the sting consumed every inch of my body. I could see cars driving past; high beams on, slowly circling the roundabout that hid my body. This is where I thought it would end. This is where I thought he would find me, finish me, kill me.

My energy, my glow, dimmed with every small rock being washed away by the rain. The pain was unbearable. My arms and legs were bruised from the fight, and my nose bleed was now a mere pink tint from the rain on my face.

One.....two.....three....four..... How many cars would pass by without noticing my white shirt glistening in their headlights. I couldn't speak, my eyes stared into the darkness, unblinking, I couldn't think. I couldn't speak. Even if I called out, would anyone hear me? Would someone help me? I closed my eyes. My mother...oh, how I missed her voice, her smell, her hair, her soft embrace when she comforted me. I drifted off for a moment in the memories.

What seemed like minutes passed and I slowly opened my eyes. I felt two arms reach under me and lift me with gentleness and power. Trying to make out who it was that had saved me, all I could sense was his rage and, in that moment, I knew.

"This is my fault, I wanted you as part of my world. I will make this right. I will protect you. I will kill him." Then...in one second, we were gone.

Contents

Chapter 1 – Friends

"Penelope! We've been waiting for over an hour! Hurry up and get down here before we leave without you!" I could hear Ronnie calling out to me, and I knew he was losing patience.

"Sorry! I'm almost ready. Just give me another minute." I was so nervous. I felt like hurling the second I heard Ronnie's voice calling up the staircase. This was it, this was the moment that Ronnie and I, and our parents and families had been waiting for—this was us finally beginning med school. Really, for the first time in our lives we would be living far away from our parents, far away from everything we knew. I had finished my undergrad at Charleston Southern University, so close to my parent's house that I could walk to school.

I had dreamed of going to Duke for as long as I could remember. My grandpa went there, and so did my mom. Now it was time for me to carry the torch. I had never thought twice about where I would go to med school because I had always assumed that my mom would be there to lead the way. She was the second doctor in her family, and I wanted to be the next.

This past year had been horrible. My dad and I lost my mom to a horrible cancer that appeared out of nowhere, six months after her diagnosis she was gone. We watched her fight until the very end, her spirit never broken. It all happened so fast, and some days I'd think about her, and other days I'd try to push the memories of her to the back of my mind. She was an angel. My angel. The beautiful angel that had made Duke a dream for me, and who had fought so powerfully through her cancer. I guess that's why God decided to take her home.

Throughout it all, my best friend Ronnie was there for me every step of the way. I don't think I could have made it through all the heartache and tragedy without him. I was so glad we had both been accepted to Duke. He and I would attend Med school together and, even though I was nervous, I couldn't wait to start this next chapter of my life.

I quickly put my admissions letter, my EarPods, and a picture of my mom and me into my bag and headed downstairs. My friends Ronnie and Lyla had come to pick me up so we could spend our weekend at orientation, meeting our roommates and getting settled in. As I made my way downstairs I could see Ronnie and Lyla in the living room with my dad.

"Come on! It's not every day that we get to have some one-on-one time with our professors. I want to make a good impression!"

Ronnie couldn't wait. There they were, my friends from elementary school. One in a Duke sweatshirt, and the other in some ripped jeans and a pink tank top.

"Pen! Lyla! You guys, this is it!" Ronnie exclaimed. "This is going to be us against the world! Only three weeks before we start on our roads to becoming doctors!"

"Okay, you are little too committed to this. It's med school not the creation of new life forms for the world, Ronnie." Lyla laughed.

"Oh, but what if it were?" Ronnie remarked.

"Let's just get these introductions over with so we can just start the festivities of being accepted to Duke, and just party our way through the first year. I'm not ready to get that serious just yet!" Lyla always had a way of creating a fun perspective even though she was super smart. She was a small thing. She always wore ripped jeans, and a bright colored tank top to match her pink and blue pixie cut. Flawless makeup and a love of shoes.

I grabbed my bag, my keys, and purse. My dad was by the door ready to see us off. "Hey kiddo. Guess it's time to see what your new world will look like, huh? Be careful, and you all just pay attention to the road". My dad tried to show no emotion.

"Thanks Dad. It's only a couple of days and I'll be back. We will have more time when I get back. I know you haven't had much time to yourself since mom…" I looked at him with a half smile and he hugged me.

"Yes Mr. Ash! We got this! Penelope is fine with us!" Ronnie yelled out.

Not sure if he would ever say it, but my dad always had one eye out for Ronnie. Ronnie was over the top, sometimes a little too over the top. His natural blonde hair was the envy of every woman, as was his thin physique. He was 5'11 and built to run. His Duke hoodie hid his muscle definition.

I felt uneasy leaving my dad at home since my mom had passed away so recently. He always said he was okay thinking about her memories, and the time they had together. Part of me knew he was keeping things to himself, but my dad always had a way of trying to make me feel comfortable about any situation. Thankfully, this was only weekend trip. What's two days?

It took about three hours from the time we loaded up in Ronnie's car to the time we were parked in front of the most wonderful and amazing university I had ever seen. The building looked just like a castle sitting among the lush trees in beautiful Durham, North Carolina. I had seen pictures of Duke of course, and had planned a trip here with mom before she got sick. She had every detail of our trip nailed down from where we would eat, to where we would stay, to meeting the Chancellor and all my instructors. She also had my residency all planned out, and the areas in which she wanted me to specialize.

I was going to be a doctor...but now, I didn't really know if I wanted that. It had been my calling for the longest time, or so I thought. But watching my mom get sick just devoured my confidence of having the heart and stomach to help others. I held resentment towards the sickness that made me lose my friend and my rock. If I couldn't face cancer, then I couldn't be the doctor I wanted to be.

"Pen! Look! I bet you've never seen sculptures like this in your life!" Ronnie was so excited to finally arrive. There were tables spread out with people handing out flyers for student groups you were encouraged to join. I could see other students with their parents sitting out on blankets eating their midday lunch. There was activity all around and animals, so many animals everywhere. Duke was nestled between lush forests, and I could hear birds chirping and see squirrels chasing each other all over the open field. This felt like a dream. A beautiful one.

"Okay, let's make this quick because I want to check out some of these places around town where all the students hang out. I heard there's a bar a block from here called, The

Port. We're not going to miss a chance to hang out and meet some locals and maybe some new blood. Right Pen? Right!" Lyla was as eager about meeting others as I was about getting settled and understanding the Duke chain of command before my first day of class in just under a month.

We met with the Chancellor and then had lunch on campus. He was a very old man but extremely intelligent. He wore a suit and had white hair combed back so that it covered his entire head like feathers on a dove. Lyla didn't seem interested in our conversation about organ transplantation. She hasn't been much interested in actually studying, she was more interested in making money. Her strict parents had forced her into studying medicine and she vehemently obliged because they were funding her studies. Her lack of commitment caused me to barely focus on Chancellor Adams and, as well, thoughts of my mother were the forefront of my brain, and all I wanted to do was get lunch over with and crawl back into our car and go home. Lunch lasted all of 90 minutes and then we were free.

"Seriously Pen, *that* was the great Chancellor you were so anxious to meet last year? Spare me, what a snooze ball!" Ronnie had been unimpressed. Although the conversation was boring, the topics were interesting. Ronnie was excited about Duke for the mere fact that he wanted to make a lot of money as an anesthesiologist. He had been offered a scholarship to study at Duke, which worked out for both of us. He definitely couldn't pass up the opportunity if it meant going to med school with his two best friends.

Lyla was ready to bust loose and she took it upon herself to organize the rest of our day, "Ok guys, this was fun and all, but now let's have some real fun! I have a friend who was living in the dorms, but she moved back in with her mom. Their place is a block from here. We can go there, get ready, and head out for the night!"

I was hesitant. "I don't know Lyla, I told my dad we would be back tomorrow night and we still haven't seen the dorms and had the tour. I don't want to stay out late and not be able to wake up early tomorrow. " I had promised Dad it would be two days and I would bring back pictures. As well, it would be kind of strange staying on campus as a graduate, and I'd rather know what's going on.

"Seriously Pen, one bar, it's Duke! We are far from home; can you just loosen up and come out this one time, please? We all know that when classes start you will be nowhere to be seen in the party scene...and you know it!" Lyla looked at me, batting her eyelashes as if that would compel me to agree.

I took a deep breath, sighed, and loaded up in Ronnie's car. We drove about five minutes and arrived at her friend's place. Lyla's friend lived in a 1,500 sq ft two bedroom apartment that had the markings of an interior designer.

"Look at this place! I mean I knew Malee's mom had an eye for taste, but damn! This looks like they hired a Hollywood designer to decorate!" Lyla exclaimed.

"Well, hello all you newbies, my name is Malee Statler and I'm here to show you the best time ever! Do you like to drink? Or maybe dance? Med school is no joke, and I guarantee by your last semester you will need a gin and tonic to go with all your research!" Malee was a party girl. Her long brown hair was tossed up in a yellow handkerchief, her dark green eyes looked sharp under all the brown eye shadow, and she wore a white mid drift tank top on with a black skirt. She wore bright yellow tennis shoes and dark lipstick.

"You can call me Mal if you want. I'm in my second semester of my MBA here at Duke and a good friend of Ly's...and who is this?" Malee pointed at Ronnie and walked over to give him a hug.

"Uh, hey. Yeah, I'm Ronnie". He looked at me with confusion.

"Hi, I'm Pen. Lyla and I have been friends since we were little".

Malee walked us to the living room. "Moooomm! Come meet Lyla and her friends!" Within a few minutes, Mal's mom came to say hi. She was the most dolled up version of a 5'8, dirty blonde, big busted Barbie I had ever seen in real life. She had a face full of make-up that looked like it had been done by a professional. I was pretty sure she's had Botox, and her pearly white teeth could light up the room.

"Look at you fascinating kids! Are you ready to start at Duke this year? You're gonna love it! Malee here is on her second year. She has a 4.0 GPA so far. I keep telling her she ought to find new friends if she wants to keep that GPA!"

New friends? She seemed like she had a good head on her shoulders. Maybe she just hung out with the party crowd. I see how that could affect her studies.

"All right, Mom, we get it. Well, gals, guy, whatever you need, bathroom is right down the hallway and my room is to the left. Go get ready and then we can go par-teee."

"You still live with your mom?" Ronnie laughed.

"You're about to find out how expensive school can be when you're trying to excel." Malee smirked. She clearly didn't know Ronnie had been accepted on a scholarship.

I politely excused myself and walked towards the bathroom. I hadn't had a chance to really freshen up since we'd arrived in Durham. I'd had to make do with quick stops in the public bathrooms. As I walked down the hall I took in the beautiful paintings on the wall and the soft lighting, but I was distracted when I saw an unusual bright light coming from a corner in one of the rooms. The light was a bright green that seemed to glow, and expand and contract. With-

PETAL

out thinking I walked towards the room. As I approached, the light grew brighter and brighter.

"Pen, dear." I felt a hand on my shoulder. "The bathroom is right over there." Malee's mom snapped me out of my trance. I took a deep breath and apologized to Mrs. Statler. I walked into the bathroom and shut the door. What was that light? Why did I feel like it had been beckoning me? Had Mrs. Statler seen it, too? I had no time to think more about this experience, and I really wanted to get out of the clothes I had been wearing. I washed my hands and generally made myself presentable. I put on a black silk shirt and jeans, and then joined everyone else in the living room.

Malee's mom brought us some snacks and drinks, and at about 9:00 pm we were all ready to go.

"Okay, everyone," Malee announced, "we are taking my ride to The Port. You are going to love that place, but it is definitely a place you don't want to be seen without a local. Let's head out!"

The four of us made our way outside, listening to the reminders from Malee's mom to be careful, drive carefully, and not be home too late. As soon as I walked outside my mouth dropped open at the sight of Malee's car sitting in the driveway.

"Meet....Shadaya. The boss of bosses," Malee said, gesturing to an orange Zenvo ST1 parked in the driveway with its engine lit, waiting for us to get in. I was completely at a loss for words. Where on Earth did her and her mom get this, what did they do to afford a car that was worth more than half a million dollars? My mind began to race. Their apartment was nice, but it was a fairly small space, and it was just them two. Were they drug dealers? Was her dad in the picture?

Lyla grabbed my hand and pulled me towards the car. "Look at this beautiful thing! This is so awesome! I've never even seen one before. Get. The. Hell. In!"

Lyla hopped into the front passenger seat and Ronnie, without hesitation, jumped into the rear seat. I slowly opened the one of the rear doors and slid in next to Ronnie. My eyes were completely wide with worry about how fast this thing could go.

"Hey, are you okay? You're really quiet." Ronnie could tell I was having a moment. "It's okay. I'm here with you. I have your back. Let's stick together and just have a good time. It'll be fun." Ronnie had a way of making me feel comfortable in the most awkward and scary situations. I felt better and kind of silly for worrying about a car. Ronnie was right, we both deserved to have a good time. Lyla turned up the music in the front seat, Malee put the car in gear and, we were off.

I fully expected we'd get pulled over because the car looked like trouble but, to my surprise, Malee was a pretty good driver. The drive was a little longer than I had expected—we took a 15-minute drive across town and then a 10-minute drive through a scenic route in North West Durham. We pulled up to a nicely lit strip of what looked like bars and restaurants. I could make out the name of the last establishment, closest to the evergreen trees, "The Port." We had arrived.

I took my hair out of my ponytail and ran my hands through it. It still smelled like my coconut shampoo from this morning, but at least the frizz was under control. Lyla got out of the car with Malee who handed her keys to the valet. Ronnie came to open my door and I took his hand and we all walked over to the end of the strip where The Port was located. I couldn't see anyone at the door.

"Is it open?" I asked Malee.

"Oh, it's open, alright. You just have to know how to get admitted." I wasn't sure knowing how to get in a place like this was something I wanted to know how to do. As I had this thought, I saw Malee fiddling with something that looked like a key and a lock mechanism.

I stood behind Lyla and whispered in her ear, "Lyla, I don't know about this".

"Oh, come on, Pen! You'll love it! *We'll* love it! Mal knows what she's doing, just trust me. This is going to be so much fun!"

"Guys, give me one sec, just let me get this thing going." We stood behind Malee at the door for almost five minutes when Malee suddenly shouted, "got it! I knew I could get it working. See. That's what happens when you're friends with Neons."

Neon? What the heck is a Neon? Neon like a crayon, or a light? What was she talking about? Malee tugged at the door and it opened, as if by magic.

As we entered, the first thing I noticed was a long black hallway lit with green and blue low lights. I could hear music coming from underneath my feet. We walked down the long hallway and came to an elevator. So far, we had not seen another person. Malee buzzed the elevator and the door opened immediately. Inside was an attendant. He looked like he was straight out of GQ magazine. His hair was slicked back and he wore a suit and tie. He directed us towards the basement level...the only floor that seemed to be available in the elevator.

Was this some kind of Speakeasy? Silently, we were transported downstairs. As soon as the door opened, the loud dance music blasted my ears. We were in the basement of The Port. It was a fancy, but large, with a bar and restaurant. There was a circular stage in the middle of the space where two bartenders were serving up drinks. Around the bar area was a massive dance floor where everyone was dancing amid the glowing lights. The Port was dark and dimly lit, it was loud, and it was pretentious.

Everywhere I looked, there were people around my age dressed in suits, cocktail dresses, and clothes you would see straight out of a Vogue magazine. This place reminded me of the Vanderpump Rules show I had seen on TV. Everyone's hair was perfectly coiffed, their bodies perfectly dressed, and they were all extremely attractive. I felt terribly underdressed and really out of place. The Port couldn't have been further from my scene. My idea of dressing up was when I had worn dress pants and a collared shirt to interview for my admission to Duke.

"All right, little heathens!" Malee exclaimed. "I promised you a fun night out." What would you like to drink?"

I had promised my mom that I would not experiment with alcohol until I had my med degree, and I wanted to keep that promise. Lyla ordered a beer and I looked at Ronnie. He immediately knew what I was thinking. He pulled me close and put his mouth to my ear so I could hear him over the loud music.

"Pen, if you don't want to drink, don't. Order a soda or something. We can always get an Uber if Malee drinks too much. No big deal. Whatever you're comfortable with."

Ronnie's words seemed to drown out and fade away amid the noise of the club.

As he was talking, I had been scanning the room and, in the middle of everyone on the dance floor, I could see the same green light I had seen at Malee's house. Only this time, there were eyes staring back at me. Wearing a black suit, he was tall with short black hair, and almond shaped eyes, his skin a light toned color. He was looking directly at me, his eyes a bright green, visible despite the darkened dance floor. He didn't smile, but his aura was something I could feel right away. It was almost as if I could feel a thick coat of armor and air surrounding me like a protective bubble. Something invisible was hugging me, longing to be with me.

After what seemed like an hour, but was probably only a few seconds, I turned back to Ronnie who was still talking in my ear. I said to him, "Yeah, sure, yeah, you're right. No, I probably won't drink and we'll see how the night ends up with Malee. Thanks Ronnie. Let's just have a good time."

Ronnie stayed by my side for the next couple of hours just talking and laughing. He had met some of Malee's friends and they all seemed to be getting along. These guys were tall, clean shaven, and they all wore well-cut suits. Their names were Nirab and Viken. What strange names — or was I just really small town? I kept sipping on my soda water to look as if I was at least enjoying myself. Ronnie checked on me every twenty minutes "Are you enjoying yourself? Are you okay, do you want to go home?" Each time I would say I was fine and let him continue making conversation with his new acquaintances.

Not wanting to seem like I was a stick in the mud, I walked towards the bar. Green lights on the floor lit up my every step. I was very impressed by these awesome light effects. As I got to the bar, I saw him. Again. Watching me. With his hands in his pockets, his black suit stood in sharp contrast to the white dress shirt he was wearing. He was definitely looking at me. His eyes seemed to be lit from inside, and had turned to a dull green. I had never seen anyone with eyes like this before. Why was light coming from his eyes? Was that normal? I glanced over to see Malee and Lyla on the dance floor sipping on some mixed drinks. They looked like they were having a lot of fun. Immersed in the music and everyone around them, they danced the night away. I looked back to see if that same guy with the green eyes was behind me. He was gone.

After I ordered another soda water I realized I needed to make a trip to the restroom. As I walked down a dimly lit hallway I was still guided by the green lights under my red heels, but now I was aware that someone was following me. At that moment, I realized no one else's feet lit up when they walked. I kept pace and got to the door that said "Women". I looked down and could see a blue light emanating from my feet. What? What was this—mood lighting? I put my hand on the door and as I was about to push it open I looked down the hallway. There he stood.

At the end of the hallway, breathing heavily, hands in fists at his sides, his eyes bright green again, he narrowed his sight towards the bathroom door. I was scared. What on earth was he doing? Terrified, I opened the door to the restroom and a blast of blue light threw me from the floor into the air.

"Penelope!" he yelled.

Then, the next thing I knew, I was sitting at a table in a semi-lit room, with *him*.

"Just listen to my voice, and focus your gaze on my eyes." With his chiseled jaw, his dark hair loosely framing his face, his eyes sharp on me, his lips commanded me. He was tall, his hands were strong, and his voice deep.

I found it almost impossible to ignore him, but managed to reorder my thoughts. What the hell happened? Why am I sitting with him, here, in this room? I was just trying to go to the bathroom!

"You're strong, Penelope..." he said, as if reading my mind.

The next moment, it seemed as if I had been transported, transported back to the present. I was flying through the air and thrown ten feet across the room. I could see a green blanket of light around me, and what should have been a bone-breaking landing was a minor blow. My head hit a side table and my vision became hazy. I saw a blast of green light charge through the bathroom door. And then I blacked out.

Chapter 2 – Ford

Oh my God. I was disoriented and my head felt like a big balloon. Ronnie was holding my head in his lap, and I could hear him yelling.

"Penelope! Penelope. Can you hear me? Somebody call an ambulance! Call 9-1-1".

"No, no ambulance. I'm fine." I tried to sit up, but fell back against Ronnie. By this time, Malee and Lyla had run up to us and both of them looked aghast, not knowing what had happened.

"What the hell happened?" Ronnie demanded. "I turned around and you were laying on the floor! You have to go to the hospital." Ronnie had a sincere and horrific look on his face. "No, no! I'm fine! Where is he? He was there, and the green...where is he?" I asked.

MELY QUAN

Ronnie and Lyla looked at me, completely mystified. They had no idea what I was talking about. Malee began to say something, but then looked in a different direction.

"I know I saw someone!...and he was over there, by the bathroom," I insisted. "He knew my name. I was sitting with him, somewhere, at a table..." I spoke frantically, wanting them to believe me. I put my hands over my aching head.

"Okay, Pen. Listen to me. You've hit your head way too hard. There was some kind of pipe explosion, apparently, in the bathroom, and you were caught up in it." While Ronnie was trying to explain what happened, Lyla helped me to a chair and got me some water. I could feel everyone starting at me. The music had completely stopped and I just wanted to go home. I felt so embarrassed and confused.

"Okay, kids," Malee said, taking charge. "I think we had better head home. There's no reason for us to stay and, since Penelope doesn't want to go to the hospital, we need to make sure she lays down for the night and gets some rest." Malee hurriedly walked us back down the hallway, up the elevator, and out of the club. The valet quickly brought her Zenvo to the front of the club.

Malee's driving was a little less careful this time, as she sped around corners and down the highway. It was as almost as if she was trying to get away from The Port as fast as she could. I was so disoriented. My body was slightly sore, and I couldn't get *him* out of my head. His eyes. My God, his eyes. They were fierce and filled with rage when I looked at him. Except, somehow, I knew that rage wasn't for me. Had I somehow blacked out, and imagined us sitting together? I clearly remembered staring at him, with his body next to me, overpowering me. His breaths and lips filling me with pure oxygen. I *know* what I saw. I *know* what I was feeling. This wasn't a dream, or a moment of hallucination. *This was real.*

I lay in Ronnie's lap on the way home, hugging his legs and feeling grateful he was there. He held me and talked to me, and I couldn't imagine a better friend. As we drove through the night, Lyla fell asleep from all the drinks she had consumed, and Malee was absurdly quiet. Through her rearview, I could see bright headlights behind us. I sat up and looked out the back window. There was a huge armored truck driving close behind us. It was black with darkly tinted windows, and it was impossible to see who was driving. As I was about to ask Malee if she knew anything about who was behind us she simply said, "His name is Ford. That's all you need to know." Malee sped down her street and when we got to her driveway she parked the car, turned off the engine and then turned around to look at Ronnie and me. The armored truck was gone.

Malee turned back to look at me, "You should really think twice about going to Duke. This will be the last time I see you guys. I can't be responsible for what happens to you if you come to Durham." Ronnie and I looked at each other dumbfounded. What was she talking about?

"Malee, what the hell are you talking about?" Ronnie was impatient.

"Just go, you three need to go! You need to leave town tonight."

At this point Lyla woke up, startled. "Whoa! Is everything okay? What's going on?" Looking out the window she said, "Oh! We are back!" After a minute or so of looking at our worried faces, Lyla knew something was wrong and that we couldn't stay at Malee's any longer. We got into Ronnie's car and drove back to campus. The drive was short, and when we arrived at our building Ronnie and Lyla began to unload their bags. We had five hours to sleep before our campus tour tomorrow morning, and then we would head back home.

Ronnie tried to help me with my bag. "It's okay, I got it. You guys head inside, I just need a minute." I wanted to just sit and think.

"Are you sure Pen? I'm worried about leaving you alone out here. You need to get some rest." I hugged Ronnie and said I would see him inside in a couple of minutes.

I sat on the curb next to Ronnie's Toyota AE86. He had worked on it for ages, and it was his baby, his pride and joy. I sat staring at the stars in the sky, trying to make sense of the night. The best I could come up with was that my over-active imagination, along with the stresses of everything that had happened over the past few months had gotten the best of me. I just needed a good night's sleep, and a decent breakfast, and I would be OK.

I stood up and leaned over to pick up my bag. As I did so, I could feel someone standing right behind me. I heard heavy breathing and the warm air of their breath on my neck and shoulder. I could see a dull green light near my feet. Immediately, I knew who it was.

"Penelope" he whispered in my ear.

I felt a surge of emotion through my body. An electric current pulsed through my face, down my neck, trickling over my chest, and in between my legs. I gasped at the sexual pulse of energy. My lips trembled. I quickly turned around but there was no one there. Still panting, I looked down the street only to see a black armored truck driving away.

"Hey!" Ronnie came running out of the dorm building. "Come inside, it's getting late." He grabbed my bag and we both headed into the dorm.

That night, I dreamed about *him*. About Ford. The way he had looked at me. The blue light emanating from the bathroom. The room and table where we had sat. The green circle around me. His hands running down my spine. "You're strong Penelope."

I woke up, gasping for air, my body shivering from the cold in my freezing room. I pulled the covers over me and fell back asleep.

The next morning, after breakfast, all three of us gathered outside our dorm, ready for the school tour. There were about 20 of us altogether; all of us looking a little *tired* and worse for wear from the night before. At 9:00 am on the dot our tour guide arrived.

"Hi everyone! I'm so so excited that you are here. My name is Hannalee and I'll be your student tour guide today. I'm a second year Duke student and absolutely *love* being a Blue Devil! As we walk around campus, I'll explain some of the amazing landmarks, where you can get delicious coffee, and lots of other information. If you have any questions, feel free to interrupt! All right! Let's head to our first stop, Perkins Library!"

The library was a couple of buildings down from the dorm, and it was the most elaborate and beautiful library I had ever seen. We walked inside and there were three floors of never-ending literature. I was in awe. I wasn't much of a reader, but to see something like this would've left anyone speechless. Hannalee gave a brief overview on manuscripts and historic briefs dating back centuries, and people had a chance to ask questions and look around.

As I was listening, my mind wandered for a minute and then, it hit me. Malee had mentioned an odd word last night. Something about a *Neon*? Maybe I could find out what that reference meant here in the library. It sounded like a historic group of some sort. Especially if knowing a Neon meant you could get into the club we were in last night. I had a few minutes as I saw the group split up and explore the different levels of the library. Ronnie and Lyla were both walking and talking about the people they had met last night. I interrupted them for a second, "Hey, guys, I'll catch up with you in a minute. I'm just going to the restroom."

I scurried away from the group and went to the library's front desk. I had no idea what I was looking for. Neon? Green lights? Hurling energy? God, would I ever be able to figure this out? I could start with Greek Mythology, or maybe something about gods. Okay, Penelope, do you actually believe this guy was a god, or from some other world? I mean, he had to be. I couldn't think of another explanation. I went over to talk to the librarian on duty. She was an older lady, but rather pretty. Nice, thin physique with bright red glasses.

"Excuse me, do you mind telling me where I can find any reference to a group maybe called the Neons, or any information about an old club called The Port?" She looked at me with suspicion in her eyes.

"No, sweetie, I'm sorry, those two names don't ring any bells." Okay, was she just too old to know about clubs, and too in the dark to understand new terminology? I dug through some Greek mythology books for a short amount of time but couldn't find anything. I decided, screw the books; I was going to Malee's to demand answers. I ran back towards Ronnie "Hey, can I borrow your car? Please, I need to do something! I'll text you when I get back and catch up with you then." Before Ronnie could say no, I took the keys from his back pocket and ran out of the library.

I raced over to Malee's house. I parked and ran out and banged on the door "Malee! Malee are you there? I need to talk to you!" Nobody answered the door. I waited for a few minutes, but still no answer. I put my hand on the doorknob and turned. It opened. Then the door shut behind me.

The small apartment was suddenly not an apartment any longer. What the hell did I get myself into. It was completely dark. As I walked further inside, there were flashes of light. Every time the light flashed I could see water on both sides of me. I was walking on a path forged through a tunnel of revolving water. It looked like those huge tanks you see at aquariums. I looked toward the end of the tunnel and saw the green light! My mind raced back to when I saw the same light in that guy's eyes, and when I was here last. I didn't feel fear; I felt a pull of energy. As I began to walk toward it I heard a voice. It sounded deep and familiar, but it was hard to hear because of the sound of the water tunnel. As I reached the end, I could see Malee's hands lighting up in the same distinctive green color I had seen before. Malee looked up at me and I gasped.

"Stop." I heard a voice. Suddenly, the water dropped all around me. The apartment was now visible, not even wet. And there he was, the man I now knew to be Ford. Dressed in a black dress shirt, tight jeans, and black shoes. I could see his muscles through his shirt. His black hair hung down one side of his face. His gaze was locked on me, but he didn't say a word.

I was transfixed.

"What are you doing here Penelope? You need to go!" Malee interrupted my reverie, grabbed my arm, and began to rush me out the door.

"No. Let her go. Now." Ford commanded in a calm but direct tone.

Turning to me he said, "My name is Ford." He extended his hand, and I reached out and touched him. Immediately, I again felt the electric charge through my body. And then I was transported.

We were in the middle of a forest, and he was undressing me slowly. Kissing my neck and shoulders. His warm lips against my skin felt arousing. As he pulled my shirt off, he gently ran his hands over my breasts.

I quickly released his hand and was transported back to Malee's apartment. I felt myself blushing, and I looked at him in confusion. What had just happened? Did I dream that, or was it real? One thing I knew was real for sure: Ford was beautiful.

"I'm Penelope," I managed to stutter, "but you already knew that."

Malee watched this exchange, and she looked very angry. "I guess I'll just wait!" She walked to her bedroom and shut the door.

"I...I had come by to talk with Malee about last night." His eyes never left mine. He was fixated on me. "I came here this morning because I wasn't sure I had the whole story about what happened to me last night. You. You were there. I saw something green and blue, and I remember us being...at..." I was losing my words. Speaking out loud I sounded crazy to myself, especially thinking about the floating water tunnel.

Ford moved closer to me. "You are not ready to understand what happened last night. Consider it a stroke of bad luck." I could smell his pheromones. They were entrancing. I breathed him in and closed my eyes. He reached up and put his hand to my cheek. "If you get hurt, I will never forgive myself. But you need to go. Now."

I opened my eyes and he was gone! What the...where the hell did he go? Now I was even more confused. I sensed Malee was mad when she walked away so I decided to wait to talk to her. I slowly walked back to Ronnie's car and headed back to campus. I had missed the whole tour and arrived just as Ronnie and Lyla were packing up.

"Where the hell did you go Penelope?" Lyla demanded. "You didn't even see their hospital or their stadium. How are you going to describe that to your dad?"

I gave her a sincere smile and said, "My head was hurting from last night. I just wanted to see if I could buy some Tylenol. I got lost and couldn't find my way back. I'm bummed that I missed most of the tour."

"Well, we got worried when you weren't back in ten minutes," Ronnie said. "How are you feeling now?"

"I feel much better. My headache is better, for sure. Sorry to have worried you guys."

I think that probably satisfied Lyla, but I wasn't sure. She was smart, and I could tell she didn't believe everything I'd said. I handed Ronnie back his keys and we grabbed our things and loaded up his car. Orientation weekend was over and it was time to go home. The drive home was a bit longer because we stopped for lunch. Ronnie and Lyla talked non-stop about their visit to Duke. I tried to appear interested in what they were saying, but I couldn't stop thinking about Ford, about his lips, his body, his voice. The way he said my name. I had never felt this way before. And, what did he mean when he said *I wasn't ready?*

Chapter 3 - His Warrior

Two weeks had gone by since my visit to Duke, since the episode at The Port, since Ford, since the green light madness. I was trying to forget the weird experiences, and was starting to feel okay with it all. I was looking forward to beginning my studies and starting this new chapter in my life.

I finished up my packing and headed downstairs to say bye to my dad for the last time before I'd see him again during Thanksgiving break. We hugged profusely, said a million I love yous and he saw me out the door to my car. Before I got into my car my dad handed me a small box. "Pen, this was your mother's. I figured it would be good to give it to you now." I opened the box and in it was a small pendant. Tears filled my eyes. I turned it around and saw a small engraving on the back, "In your darkest fears I will appear." I wasn't sure what it meant but I looked up and thanked my dad.

Ronnie and Lyla were parked outside in their cars, ready to caravan to Duke. Dad and I finished the final bit of packing up my old white Lancer.

"I'll lead the way, Pen you follow, and then Lyla will be our caboose! Let's get on with it!" Ronnie yelled. Lyla looked over at him and started to laugh.

I loved my car as much as Malee loved her Zenvo. I had gotten her back in 2009, and she still ran like a beauty. It was my first car, the place I had my first kiss, where I'd had my first accident, she was the owner of many firsts. Just, not *that* first. I was saving that first for someone truly special. Someone I could see myself with throughout my entire life. I hugged Dad one last time, started the engine, and headed off on the four-hour drive to Duke.

Once we arrived, the first thing we had to do was find out which rooms we had been assigned, and then unload our stuff. This should be fun; I was going to meet my roommate today. They assigned us the same roommate for a full year so I was crossing my fingers for someone normal. Unfortunately, Lyla had signed up too late in the process and wasn't able to be my assigned roommate. Lyla headed inside to meet her advisors while Ronnie took off to meet his new roommate.

I was assigned Room 617 and when I got there the door was closed. Seemed kind of odd since the dorm was crowded with new students moving in, and there was a lot of noise and laughter and people running in and out of rooms. I knocked on the door.

"Come in!" I heard a voice call out, and my first thought was that Barbie was my roommate.

I opened the door and walked in. To my amazement, there were pink lights, pink curtains, pink bedposts, and a pink lamp all adorning the half of the room belonging to my roommate. I let out a tiny groan.

"Hi!" she said. "You must be Pen, I'm Velaire!" Seriously, where did these names come from? Nirab, Viken, and now Velaire? Maybe I just needed to be exposed to more things.

"Hi, Ve-l-aire. Yes, I'm Pen. Glad to meet you".

"Hm, well, you and I are going to have a lot of fun this year" Velaire giggled.

"I can't wait." I half smiled.

"Well! Make yourself at home! Hope my pink vibe doesn't bother you. Love the color and the two colors that make pink..." Her eyes squinted at me.

I smiled and went about setting up my half of the room. It took me most of the day. I hadn't even stopped to eat lunch. I could hear my stomach growling. I looked down at my watch. It was almost 7:00 pm. Holy cow! I'd lost track of time. I decided I had done enough decorating and redecorating - I always had a small case of OCD.

I left my dorm and headed towards a strip of restaurants. It was already dark but the campus had a lot of lighting. I got to a place called Handy Sandwich. I was hungry, figured I could eat, and go back to my dorm to get some real sleep. There was a long line, but once I got my sandwich I sat down to eat. I ate really slowly, and by the time I left it was about 8:30 pm. Before going back to my dorm, I decided to explore a little since I had missed half the tour at orientation. There was the hospital, the stadium, so many places here I hadn't seen. I figured I would give the stadium a try. At this hour, there are not too many people to run into at the stadium. I started to walk in that direction. I hadn't realized the size of the campus. After about ten minutes I was able to see the entrance. The lights must have been out because the entrance to the stadium was blacked out minus a few lights turned on inside. As I made my way to the front, I could hear swooshing sounds behind me. I quickly turned around but nothing was there. I kept walking and heard the sound again. This time I turned around and there in front of me, floating in the dark sky, was a figure. It was a man with a dark cloak, red eyes, a defined jawline, and the whitest teeth I had ever seen. As he smiled, he floated down to the ground in front of me. He wore an armored vest and black pants. He was of medium-build and had a gentle but sly tone.

"Hi. You must be new? What are you doing over here by the stadium?"

I couldn't answer his questions. Part of me was in shock, but the other part knew better than believe a man in a black cloak had just floated over me and landed in my path. Just then, another floating figure came behind me. He too had on a black armored vest and was of medium-build. He seemed more impatient and angry. I started to panic.

"Give us what you have and there will be no need to worry." The second man's voice was forceful.

What the hell did I have that they could possibly want? I was confused and afraid.

"Yeah, listen to him. We don't need him getting angry, or this won't end well for you!" said the first man. They both moved in closer. I could feel their body heat. They were radiating so much heat from their bodies that if I were to touch them I would be scorched. "Come on. It will only last a minute. You'll like it."

One of them reached for my jean pocket. "You know you want to. That power inside of you is dying to spill out." At that moment, an enormous flash of green light powered through one of the cloaks throwing him against the stadium wall and shattering him to pieces. I ducked for fear of landing in the crossfire. Another green laser of energy, and the second cloak was demolished. I lay on the ground with my hands over my head. My heart was pounding and I was immovable with fear.

"Penelope! Are you okay? Did they do anything to you?" I was too afraid to look up. "Answer me! Did they touch you?"

"No!" I yelled! Ford looked down at me as I shook with terror. He reached out for me and lifted me up off the ground.

"Come with me. I'll take you somewhere safe. Don't worry, I will protect you." Ford quickly walked me to his car conveniently parked on the side of the stadium. Wow. His armored truck was amazing. It looked like a truck I had seen in a magazine once. I think the name of it was a Karlmann King. At least that's what it looked like. He opened my door and hoisted me into the passenger's seat. He hurried past the front and got in and we sped off into the night. He was driving fast, extremely fast. I wanted to say something but what was I going to say? Thank you? "How did you know I was here? Were you following me? You need to calm down." He was breathing heavily and focused on the road.

"How can I calm down?" he asked. "Why were you even out there, alone, at this time of night? You don't know what they could've done to you! What they wanted with you!"

"Do to me? What do you mean? What is going on? How do you know?" I was anxious and felt helpless. I needed help but, out of all people on campus, it had to be Ford?

"That doesn't matter right now. The point is that you're safe and I have you." He started to slow his breathing.

"How did you know I was at the stadium? Have you been following me?" I retorted.

"No! Yes. Sort of. Look, I'll explain when we get to my house."

His house? Where exactly was he taking me? He had just saved my life, but I wanted answers. We sat in silence as he drove for what seemed like an hour. Eventually, we pulled up to a wooded area. "We're here. Penelope, come, trust me." He extended his hand. I reached over and grabbed it. Instantly, we were transported. It felt as if I was riding through a long underground tunnel for a few seconds. He let go of my hand and we had been transported in front of a door seemingly located underground. He pushed the door open and we were inside a fortress. The inside of the house was all on one level, but it was huge. It was adorned with glass figures, glass desks, glass chairs, glass frames. Everything....glass. Of different colors.

I inhaled deeply, and exhaled nervously. "Okay. I'm not going to act like this is not something weird. What is that thing you do when you hold my hand? I know it's real and I want to know what the hell that is. It's like you teleport me somewhere."

Ford let out a chuckle and grinned. "That's *not* teleportation. It's a little more advanced than that." He walked towards me and guided me to a white sofa with green pillows and asked me to sit down. "I will tell you what you want to know."

I sat down on the enormous feather couch. I was so tired, but I was here to get what I needed to know. I wanted him to tell me who those two men were, and what they wanted with me. Ford slowly moved over and sat next to me, his eyes fixed on my every move. It was almost as if he was studying me. He sat down hunched slightly forward, with his elbows on his thighs and his hands interlocked between his legs, looking at me. God. He looked entrancing. I couldn't help but stare at him. His hands were strong. He slowly removed his blazer. He wore a fitted shirt underneath. His arms flexed as he poured some water into a cup and handed it to me. I licked my bottom lip and took the cup of water and slowly took a drink.

"So, how did you know where I was?" I stumbled to get my words out. Ford moved closer to me. His knee touched my leg. I felt him - I felt his power.

"Penelope, ever since I saw you at The Port, I've been keeping an eye on you. I haven't been able to get you out of my mind. I have a strong urge to protect you, and to shield you from what's coming."

I was confused and overwhelmed. "What do you mean, 'what's coming'? I asked. "What is this whole thing you do to me when I touch your hands? Did I imagine this? I don't understand."

Ford took my hands in his. "No. It's real. Penelope, what you've seen is real. It's a....thing I can do...with my mind. My power. I'm...what you call a Neon. I can project ideas and memories into your head and make it seem as if you are somewhere else, but only your mind is there. Your body stays here, in the present. I can also teleport you if I want, but that takes a strong person to go through that. I also have to touch you to do that. I projected an idea into your mind while at The Port, and shielded you with my power. I didn't want you to be traumatized; I didn't want you to know. It all happened so quickly your friends didn't even see any of it."

My eyes watched his lips as he talked. He waited for a response as my eyes moved up to his and were locked. My lips were quivering, trying to understand. "Are you human?" I asked.

"Yes, sort of. Except, I have special abilities. A Neon is someone who has an energy field they can control by harnessing inner power. We can channel it to do practically anything we want it to do. Some of us have very distinct powers that can insert memories into your mind, teleport you, or conjure a thrust to hurt your enemies." Ford responded.

"Enemies?" I looked up at Ford as he turned away. "Ok, then what about at Malee's apartment?" I blushed at the thought of him undressing me.

"Penelope, I'm drawn to you. To your mind, your voice, your body. Ever since I saw you at The Port I haven't been able to stay away from you. I want you. Not in the way you think, but you'll know soon. There is something about your aura, it pulls me to you."

I was shaking. His voice made me tremble throughout my body. It was arousing. I cleared my throat and, in a low tone, I asked "So, where do Neons come from?"

Ford began to move his lips but instead of explaining he said, "Let me show you. Take my hand."

I was hesitant. Every time I took his hand I felt out of control, out of my own mind, but somehow I was unable to resist him. I slowly and reluctantly extended my hand and he slid his fingers in between mine. He transported us to an open field with a castle in the distance. We walked towards the front door. It opened and we walked inside. Inside I could see soulful sculptures — a dragon breathing fire holding a body in its talons — a big creature with long pointed ears and muscular legs — a gargoyle in flight across the top of a pool of what looked like blood? The sculptures were horrific. What did they mean? Whose house was this?

"I come from a line of warriors and protectors born with distinctive powers. One of my powers is being able to mend minds, the other is an electric charge I can conjure with my body and mind, and force the energy through my hands...and other things...but you've seen it. At the stadium...I hope I didn't scare you." He turned to look at me and pulled me closer to his body. My breasts almost touching his chest.

I looked up at him. "No, I'm not scared. You don't scare me." He let me go and we were transported back to his couch.

I was breathing heavily. Getting close to him made me feel out of control. He made me feel like I could let my guard down—like I had no guard. He made me feel as if I didn't have to be in the driver's seat all the time. We sat on his couch and he offered me some wine. I hesitated. "Penelope, you are safe here. It's okay. I won't harm you. I just want to protect you."

I looked at him. What was wrong with me? I had a rule of not drinking, but school wasn't starting for another few days. Maybe I could do this while I didn't have to worry about any schoolwork. I was undoubtedly stressed, and

perhaps I needed to chill out and put all the recent trauma-
tizing events aside for the evening. Besides, technically, I
had sipped on some champagne last year at New Years, so
why not?

We talked for what seemed like hours into the night. We
talked about why I had chosen to go to Duke. About my
friends Ronnie and Lyla and how close I was to them. I
didn't bring up my mom or dad. I felt it wasn't the right
time just yet to talk about my parents. By the time we were
done I'd had two glasses of wine and was starting to feel
tipsy.

"Are you okay?" Ford served me a glass of water, sensing that I didn't need any more alcohol.

"Yes, yes, I'm fine. Maybe I'll just lay off some of the
wine. We've talked about literature, my studies, my friends,
but what about you? I want to ask you some more questions." Ford looked at me with his sharp green eyes.

"Ask me anything. I'll give you the answer." He was a
rather serious person and his eyes had so much to tell.

"Those two men in black cloaks..." I could see his eyes
filling with rage." They asked me to give them something,

but I can't understand what they wanted. Why were they after me?"

Ford stood up and walked towards the fireplace. He grabbed some lighter fluid, poured it on the wood, struck a match and the dark room lit up. The wooden logs roared and caught on fire. I could smell it. A cinnamon flavor. It smelled good. "You don't need to know that right now, Penelope."

I was growing impatient. "Okay, you somehow show up when I'm about to be blasted into obliteration, you follow me for days and stalk me, you show up at a stadium and completely crush two men in cloaks, you get inside my head and lead me here, and you *don't* want to answer my question? You said I could ask you anything!"

Ford walked over and took my hand. He pulled me close and my body was pressed against his. My breasts were crushed against his chest, his leg was between both of mine, and his hands cupped my face. I couldn't move, I couldn't pull away. But I didn't want to. He leaned in and put his lips on mine. A second later let me go and then looked at my hands. I looked into his eyes. What was he doing?

He was breathing heavily and I could see that he was aroused and he wanted me. I opened my mouth to ask him but, again, he took me in his arms and kissed me feverishly. I pushed him away. "Ford, what are you doing? I asked you a question. I...I'm not used to doing things like this." He looked at me with desire in his eyes.

"Penelope, I'm sorry, I know. I just wanted to show you the answer to your question." Seeing the confusion on my face, he asked, "Do you trust me?"

"Yes," I said in a low shivering tone. He made me feel things I had never felt before. The longing in his eyes sent electricity running through my mind and body. I did trust him, but I couldn't explain why.

"Come to me." Ford looked at me, his green eyes glowing. He took me and held me close again. Taking some of my hair, he pulled my head back, and began kissing my neck. I began to moan and breathe heavily. My body wanted this. I could see a dull pink light emanating from below us. What was he doing? I could feel Ford's heart racing. With my neck exposed he began kissing my collarbone.

PETAL

"Ford, I have to tell you something," I stammered. I felt I should tell him to stop but the truth was I didn't want him to stop. He took my hands and pinned them behind my back, then pushed me against the wall with his body. He began kissing my chest and slowly making his way down to my breasts. Restraining me. It felt...so good. "Ford, stop!"

In that moment, he quickly pulled away. My chest was heaving, and my emotions were flaring.

My hands...my hands! They were glowing, surrounded by an electric pink charge. Electricity was flowing from my hands. I was in shock... "Ford! What did you do to me? What is this?" I was frantic.

"This power is the answer to your question, Penelope. Your rage, your power, your innocence is revealed by this light. *This* is what they wanted."

But, how could this be? How did this even happen? What power! I didn't have any power! I was now more confused than ever. I began to shake.

"Penelope, it's okay. You're going to be fine. There is just a lot you don't know. Possibly a lot your mother wasn't able to tell you before she passed away."

My mother? "How do you know any of this? Why would you bring my mother into this conversation? I need to go. I need to leave. Take me home now!" Ford took my hand and led me back out to his armored truck.

We pulled up to my dorm and sat quietly in the car. "Penelope, I...."

"Ford, not...right now. I need some time." I opened the door and got out. I didn't look back. I couldn't stand to look at him and be forced to see his fierce eyes and strong face luring me back.

I got to my room and opened the door. It was already 1:00 am. I snuck inside so as not to wake Velaire. She had fallen asleep listening to a white noise machine playing sounds of crashing waves. I was completely torn with everything I had discovered tonight. My heart hurt and I couldn't get my mom out of my head. The white noise was soothing. I climbed into my bed and fell asleep to the sounds of the ocean.

PETAL

Chapter 4 - The Siren

I awoke the next morning to Velaire's loud music playing "I Shot the Sheriff" by Bob Marley. I had a deep
headache from all the events the night before, and all the
uncertainty and fear came rushing back to the forefront. I
just wanted to stay in bed and sleep all day, but I had
promised my friends I would be with them today. I figured
I should go find Lyla and Ronnie. Velaire was busy painting her nails but I asked her to come along in hopes we
would find some breakfast first.

Velaire and I made it to the campus breakfast hall. As I
walked to find seating I could see Lyla waving me down.
"Pen! Pen! Oh my God! Where were you all day yesterday? Ronnie and I spent the whole day signing up for different reading and research groups!" Lyla sounded like she
hadn't seen me in weeks. It was so good to see her and
Ronnie.

"Hi Penelope...good to see you made it through the night...is this your new roommate?" Ronnie remarked and looked at Velaire.

"I am. I'm Velaire! So glad to meet you two! Penelope mentioned she had two best friends here at Duke! We didn't get to talk much because she came in fast and furious, and left just the same last night."

Ronnie looked at her and then at me with confusion. Why would he say it was good to see I made it through the night? Did he know something? Maybe he saw me with Ford? I hope not. I knew that wouldn't fair well. Ronnie and I had some history. He and I were childhood best friends, but he had also been my first kiss. My first kiss in my Lancer. Except, after that kiss, our friendship took a turn and we stopped talking for almost three years.

We had been in our first year of high school and had gone on the type of date you would think two 15 year olds would go on - dinner and a movie together. He told me he liked me and we kissed during the movie. Four months into our relationship he cheated on me and kissed another girl. I found out after she confronted me. I never returned his calls or his texts, and ran in circles in my mind about what

I could've done wrong or better. I later realized that he wanted more. I wasn't open to anything more than kissing at the time. We were young. Three years went by and we finally connected again the last semester of our senior year. We never spoke about what happened and just left it behind and became friends again.

I walked through the breakfast line getting my usual banana, cereal, toast, and coffee. My biggest meal was always in the morning, and my appetite would dwindle down towards the evening. Lyla and Ronnie grabbed some breakfast and sat down at a table. Lyla started talking about the different fields she potentially wanted to study while in med school. Velaire began to laugh. "You do know if even you don't give it that much thought and pass you're *still* going to be a doctor" I loudly gulped down a sip of orange juice.

"Okay, Valerie or Velaire, whatever your name is, what are you into?" Lyla retorted. "Oh, well, I'm living on campus because I moved here from Italy, and Duke just so happens to offer housing for graduates from a different country. I love to party! had a great undergraduate experience and am now just continuing the family tradition!" Velaire smirked. "How did you three get accepted to live on campus, anyway?"

"Well, Pen's mom..." Lyla started. Ronnie shook his head and rolled his eyes. Suddenly she changed the subject. "So, Pen, what did you do yesterday?" I looked at Ronnie with a blank stare "I...I just." Trying to get the words out I looked over at the door as Malee walked in with a tall, red-headed girl. The redhead was toned, she had on a pair of ripped jeans, a loose silk blouse, and wore glasses.

Lyla yelled out for them to join us for breakfast. I hadn't spoken to anyone, including Lyla, about what had happened at Malee's house some weeks ago, and as Malee walked over to our table I hoped she wouldn't bring it up. She and I knew the secret, but nobody else did. But I couldn't help wondering if Malee's friend knew anything.

"Hey Lyla, Ronnie, Penelope...this is Sarina." The red-head glanced over at me in a questioning way. "She's here for her MBA, too. Working hard like me."

"Hi there. And you are?" Sarina pointed at Velaire.

"I'm Vel! Short for Velaire...I'm good with either name."

Velaire also seemed to be hooked on the redhead's beauty. I couldn't help but notice her perfect posture and extremely perky breasts visible underneath her blouse. Were they real? They were big, that's for sure. She wore perfect make-up, a far cry from the time I had worn a little blush, gloss, eyeliner, and mascara for my cousin's wedding.

"Do you guys want to join us?" I asked. And at that *exact* moment I heard Ford's voice, *"Penelope, can we talk?"* He was in my head, he was talking to me, but only I appeared to be able to hear him. He must be close by. I needed to leave. I took a last bite out of my toast and stood up from the table. "Look, I'm sorry everyone. I have to go. I've got a couple of things to do, but I will catch up with you later."

Malee looked at me inquiringly. She knew.

I hurried out of the breakfast area and began walking in the direction I felt a distinct energy pulling me. And there he was, looking at me. Leaning against the wall of the medical sciences building. He was dressed in a collared shirt and jeans that hugged him. He wore black glasses and his hair was styled back. My heart began to flutter. But I honestly didn't know how I felt about him. He was someone I was physically attracted to, but I couldn't start something with someone based on that alone. I needed to get to know him. That's if I still wanted to, and if last night wasn't some crazy dream. I assumed he didn't know I was a virgin, but I wasn't sure. But I did know that guys like him would run away from girls like me once they found out. And then there was the comment he had made about my mother. I shook my head. What the heck did that mean?

I stormed over to where he was standing. I was mad. "What were you doing last night? What the hell was that? You did something to me and I need you to undo it!" The more I talked, the more angry I became, "And, then, bringing up my mom! Come on!"

"Look, Penelope, I'm sorry. That was out of line. I shouldn't have said anything about your mother. I'm sorry...as for what happened last night, that wasn't me. That energy, that light emanating from your hands, that was all you. I...I just brought it out of you..."

I couldn't take anymore cryptic comments. "What do you mean brought it out of me?" I was yelling now and I'm sure people could hear me halfway across the campus.

MELY QUAN

"Can we go somewhere a little more private, and talk?" Ford was uneasy.

"Fine! My dorm is right over there, we can go talk in my room." I led the way.

We arrived at my room, and as he walked in he chuckled. "Wow, your roommate *loves* pink." I ignored that comment and told him to sit down so we could talk.

"Okay, I need answers. Tell me. How did you bring this out of me, how did you know I had this in me?" He didn't say anything for a few minutes and I watched him look at his watch a few times. What was he waiting on? Why was he worried about the time?

"Okay. I'm hoping you're going to believe me," he said, not looking confident. I nodded for him to get on with it.

"Penelope, as I started to mention before, I come from a long line of ancient protectors. Neons can control minds and bodies, but they can also sense things. We can sense when there is a power in our midst. We can tell if that power is dark or light, if it's male or female, if they are a Neon or not...

"When you were at The Port, I could feel you even before you walked in. I felt your emotions, your energy, and your reservations. I could feel a lot of you, and I could sense that, well, you too were a Neon."

I began to laugh. I wasn't sure why I was laughing. Maybe because me being a Neon sounded crazy! My father was a regular real estate agent, and my mother had died from cancer. How on earth could any of what he was saying be true? I couldn't be more ordinary. Besides, my parents never mentioned anything about other worldly beings, let alone Neons. They didn't even like Sci-Fi.

"I know it sounds unbelievable Penelope." I shook my head in agreement. "But you said you trusted me, and I can prove what I'm saying is true."

Prove it? How was he going to do that? Take a hair sample and send it off for DNA analysis to see if I was part of some futuristic bloodline? I held my tongue and sat thinking about Ronnie and Lyla, and what they were doing with Malee, Sarina, and Velaire. I remembered something I wanted to ask Ford about Malee.

"Ok, fine. Let's assume I believe what you're saying about me being a Neon. What about Malee? Is she one, too? I saw that her hands were green."

Ford looked at me with slight dismay. "Malee is not a blood Neon. Her and I..."

Before he could say anything else I interrupted. "Don't tell me! You and Malee are an item...you are together? Is that why she stormed off when I was at her apartment? Did she see where you transported me?" Besides being mad, now I was annoyed.

"No, no she didn't see what I projected into your mind. And...yes. Her and I *were* something. I ended it the night before you came to The Port." He seemed stoic, but I sensed his emotion. Maybe he was right—maybe that's why I could feel and sense things around me. I had always ignored those feelings, thinking it was my way of process-ing and internalizing other's behaviors towards me. "So, she is not a Neon?" I could feel a small burn of jealousy.

"No, she's not a Neon..."

"Then why were her hands glowing green that day at her apartment?" He didn't want to tell me, but I wasn't about to let the question go. "I saw her with the same green light as you. I saw her see me!"

"Yes, I know. Neons have the power of a green charge that can obliterate anything in its path if channeled correctly. I was teaching Malee how to harness some of that power." He looked at his watch again.

"Okay, well, if she's not a Neon *how* did she get that green electric aura coming from her hands? And why do you keep looking at your watch?" He could tell I was losing patience.

"It's hard to explain, Penelope. Maybe we can finish this conversation tomorrow. I need to take care of something. I've gotta go. Please trust me." He took my hand and kissed it. I had so much to ask, so much to know. Every time he kissed me I was speechless, paralyzed. I let him leave and I stayed in my room. I wanted to think about what Ford had told me.

About an hour later my phone rang. It was Lyla. She and Ronnie had been waiting for me in the campus park to go buy books. I put my shoes on and ran over to meet them. "So, Malee and Sarina, how were they? Where are they?"

Lyla took my hand and handed me a list of books. "They were great! Such cool people. Not sure they liked you much, though." I raised my eyebrows at her. "I'm kidding, I'm kidding! They wanted to spend more time with you!"

But, Lyla was probably right. They probably did hate me. I mean, if they were friends, Malee had probably told her about that night, in her apartment, with Ford.

I spent the next part of the afternoon at the school's bookshop located in the basement of the student center picking up Medical Theory, Biology, Medical Malpractice Laws and all these books I had zero desire to read. I was wrapped up in recent events, and diving deeper into studying medicine kept bringing memories of my mother to the top of my mind. I still couldn't fathom the thought of becoming a doctor. Not with the constant reminder of my mom in every facet of my life. I wanted to quit med school. I wanted to be in the workforce with the rest of my good friends, distracted by every day work. What would my dad say? Would he approve? Would he keep paying my tuition? I just wanted to focus on something other than what would remind me of my mom every day of my life. I hadn't come to terms with her illness and, frankly, I wasn't ready. I wanted to focus my time on escaping those thoughts.

I wanted to be more like Ronnie had been so far throughout the start of the semester. Ronnie was going to help people feel less pain. He'd wanted to be an anesthesiologist ever since he had undergone surgery for a broken foot from playing football. He said he loved the loopy feeling he had felt before passing out. Lyla was studying to be a spinal surgeon, and me...well, there was a lot to decide in the next few years. As we picked up our books and headed to the register I suddenly felt an eerily strong sensation through my temples, my eyes, and the front of my head. I froze.

Ronnie was standing next to me and he must have seen the strange look on my face. "Pen, are you okay? Pen!" He yelled my name. I shook my head and released the ringing in my ears. I composed myself in mere moments and then we all heard a loud noise and the lights went out in the bookstore. It was pitch black. We could see nothing but the faint red Emergency Exit lights. Everyone began to talk all at once.

"Great! Now what? This is ridiculous. Maybe this means we get our books for free!" I could hear Lyla rustling in the dark.

"Wait a minute. I should have a flashlight in my backpack," Ronnie responded.

"Yeah, okay, good. Too bad you don't have a backup generator in there," Lyla chuckled.

Ronnie pulled out a small flashlight and turned it on. He started to shine it across the room and at that point we realized we were the only people in the bookstore. What the hell? Where had everyone gone? "Give me that flashlight!" I demanded.

I grabbed the flashlight from Ronnie and started to walk around the bookstore away from Ronnie and Lyla. I slowly shone the light across the room, trying to find the entrance. As the light scanned around the room, I lit up a dark shadowy figure standing by the door. Its back was turned to me, and it was growling. I could see a blue light shining in front of it.

Oh my God. My hands began to glow pink. I tried to brush the color away but the light protruded through the darkness. A sense of evil washed over my body. I felt like I was absorbing the energy from the figure in front of me. Suddenly, it turned around and I could see it was a female, and her eyes were emitting a blue light. Her face looked burned and her skin was peeling off the side of her face. Her hands were dirty and her fingernails were black. She had thick blue saliva running down the side of her mouth. She looked at my hands and then locked eyes with me. I froze. She let out a loud growl and charged towards me. I started to backtrack and tripped over a lower shelf. I grabbed hold of a coat rack. My hands burned right through it. She jumped on top of me and I tried to hold her back. My hands burned through her chest. She let out an ear-wrenching scream.

"PEN!" I could hear Ronnie yelling.

My mind was suddenly transported to an open field. Everything was dead. Dead grass, dead trees, everything dark and brown. The stench of the air thick with the smell of blood. I tasted blood in my throat. I gagged and began to cough. A few feet away stood Ford.

"Ford. What is going on! You can't do this to me here. There's a...!" I tried to explain but he knew what was happening.

"Penelope. Focus on my voice. Focus on your mind, your emotions, your energy, your desires. Your power is fueled by those four pillars. Only then you'll be able to channel what you have to do to protect yourself."

Okay...okay. Sounds ridiculous! Where was I supposed to start?! Mind - I focused on my father. His strong demeanor. His drive for his career and the way he loved his family. He was my role model. Emotions - an image of my mother. Her smile. So real and untouched. A tear fell from my eye. Energy - I thought about Ronnie and Lyla. The fun and high-spirited friends that were always there to protect me. Desire - my mind was about to go to Ford, but I stopped. I could only think about the blast at The Port. In that instant I came back to my senses and as the pink glow from my hands overpowered the demon, the glow began to fade...what was happening? Why was it going away? The demon put her hand over my mouth and began to suck the air out of my body. I could see a red electric charge exude from my mouth into her hand. What lasted less than three seconds seemed like hours. I began to feel chills, my body started to feel stiff, and my hands fell to my sides.

"No!" Ford charged through the darkness and grabbed the demon by her riddled hair. He put his other hand around her neck and with a jolt of green energy, crushed her to pieces. I lay on the floor half-breathing. I could see Ford and could hear Ronnie and Lyla in the distance. They were yelling for me, but I couldn't say anything. Ford ran over to me and carried me in his arms, my head fell against his chest. I could feel him carrying me and hear him..."Penelope, please. Hang on. We're almost there. I can fix this. I can fix you."

What seemed like moments later, I slowly opened my eyes. I wasn't sure how long I had been out. I looked around and could see a well-lit room with ancient markings on the walls. I was in a large bed with silk sheets and a down-filled comforter nestled in my arms. Where was I? I turned towards the door and could see Ford walking in. Beside the door was a huge statue with fangs and large wings. I knew where I was. Back in the castle. With the creepy statues...

"Penelope. You're awake. How is your head, how are you feeling? You're safe now. You're in The Kingdom."

I tried to sit up, but could feel a painful bruise on the side of my head.

"Ouch." I laid back down as Ford sat next to me. I shook my head and stared at my hands.

"Who was she, that demon? " I was confused and despite my discomfort, I needed answers.

"Penelope. I'm sorry I wasn't there sooner. That girl...that creature you saw. She wasn't a demon, she was a Siren. A Siren cast off by her own kind. This happens when they break the peace that Sirens are supposed to have within their world. She was foraging for new blood when she saw you. Your power brings them here. It brings them all here." Ford exhaled.

"Ford, what do you mean 'brings them all here'? Who here?" I still didn't understand it. My mind was desperately trying to make sense of it all.

"Penelope, I still haven't told you a lot of things. I cut our conversation short at your dorm because you and I together...we are easier to hunt down."

71

"Hunt?" I exclaimed.

He interrupted, "I want you to know what you're up against. I want you to be able to protect yourself when I'm not there...I feel guilty I wasn't there for you in time. I will not leave your side unless absolutely necessary." I watched his lips move and could smell his scent creeping over me. I inched closer to him and looked in his eyes.

"I need you to tell me everything. Tell me the truth." I demanded.

Chapter 5 – Exploration

Ford took my hands and held them close to his heart. He didn't say one word, only stared into my eyes for what seemed like minutes. He started to talk to me about the four pillars.

"Energy, Emotion, Mind, Desire. These four pillars were used in our warrior days as signals. Each pillar belonged to a female Neon, who was greatest at evoking these qualities within herself.

Energy - her name was O'rien. She had long blonde hair, crystal blue eyes, fair skin, freckles all across her cheeks. She could harness magic and electric pulses like no other Neon could. She fought daily battles sparing her challengers. Her charges were too great to be defeated. Ultimately, it was her compassion that led to her death. She fell into a trap set by a group called the Temulus and they killed her."

"But if you said her power was too great, how did they kill her?" I asked.

"She had fallen in love with a Temulus. They found out, took him and the baby while they were alone. They gave her an ultimatum...give up her power and be killed, or they would kill her only newborn son. "

"And what happened to the baby?"

"He lived. The Temulus named him Griff and banished him from their world after the rest of the group found out what he was. I've only seen him once before…a few years ago."

I looked at him with shock.

"Emotion - her name was Crimson. She had short curly brown locks, big brown eyes, soft hands, and tan skin. When the Neons went to war with the Temulus, she had gone through too much and, in the end, couldn't control her rage."

"What happened?" I asked.

"The four pillars were instructed to each have a male partner throughout their lifetime in order to reproduce and bring more female Neons into the world. Well, Crimson fell in love with Sarah. Neons ended up killing Sarah for not abiding by the rules set forth in the Neon world. Neons were meant to procreate and not fall in love with the same sex. They needed to reproduce to keep the female bloodline going. Crimson destroyed everything in her clan, set everything on fire, and went down with it. She killed hundreds of people."

This all terrified me. Why would anyone do these things? Was this really in my blood? Was I really a Neon?

"Mind - Danita." He looked down and shook his head. "Danita was the most well-spoken, intelligent, and strategic of them all. Rightfully so, she led with her mind. Her emotions and power never clouded her judgment. She was my partner. My partner in strategizing how to defeat the Temulus."

Ford stopped and took a deep breath.

"Ford, it's all right if you don't want to talk about it now, but I'm here for you if you do." I slowly responded.

Ford took the soda water he had brought in for me and chugged half the glass.

"Penelope, it's fine. I'm okay...Danita died protecting me. The Temulus leader came looking for me when he knew I also had the power to mend minds and project memories. There were only two Neons that could do that: Danita...and me. Together, we were a really dangerous threat. We defeated and killed thousands of their creatures. Being able to project into one's mind to make them think they're elsewhere is a powerful thing."

"So what happened to her?" I could feel Ford's heart slow to a near drum.

"Danita...she...sacrificed herself for me. The Temulus leader at the time, Horatio, had a very distinct ability. The Temulus were descendants of ruby magic. Horatio could shield his mind from anything. It was just him one night. He caught Danita and me off guard while we were...you know."

"Okay, I get it. Yep, got it!" I retorted with an annoying tone.

"He had a powerful weapon, a talisman, that could absorb our energy and channel it through him. It made him extremely powerful. He blasted an electrifying surge and Danita used her mind to absorb it. I quickly took advantage and snapped his neck from behind. The talisman fell but before I could try and do anything, it was too late. The talisman's power was too great and Danita died..." Ford paused.

"I'm so sorry Ford. I'm so sorry you had to go through that. It seemed like she meant a lot to you." I gave him a few seconds before I had more questions.

"Ford, you mentioned ruby magic. What exactly does that mean?" I needed to know.

"Ruby magic is the single most raw and pure form of evil power that exists in our world. Only those of pure darkness and a black soul are able to harness it and control it." He stopped and looked at his hands. He was thinking and I could tell it wasn't anything good.

"Do...you...know of anyone...or thing that could have ruby magic?" I asked nervously.

"Yes. One." Ford inhaled and exhaled.

I stared at him for several minutes trying to cope with all the information he was giving me. When had I gone from a simple girl signing up for med school to a full-blown power yielding monster? I mean, was I creature? Okay, or maybe a witch? No, that didn't sound accurate. A wizard? Were wizards even real? At this point, I would say anything from the fantasy world was not off limits. I guess I'd have to stick with the title Neon. Which brought me to ask about the last pillar. Desire.

"Penelope, desire is the trickiest, but most fulfilling of them all." Ford chuckled a little. "Her name was Xela. She was a sex goddess who loved both men and women. Her power came from exploring her sexuality and channeling it through the strongest practices that gave her pleasure. She died during our war with the Temulus."

I couldn't help but wonder if Ford had slept with her too...or tried to. I shook my head to relieve my thoughts.

"Penelope, for years, the four pillars tried to conceive a female Neon to pass on their powers, but they couldn't. To the three that tried, three sons were born. All as a rightful heirs to the power of our world.

"Why were Neons so concerned about birthing girls? I mean, normally, it's the boys they want because they carry on their legacy, they take their rightful place on thrones, in leadership roles, etc, etc." I began to ramble. I could see Ford's eyebrows raise a little as he looked at me with wonder.

"Okay, so I take it gender roles are some kind of trigger for you? I get it. A girl was preferred because there was a time when we tried to live civil with the Temulus. They had power over us in ways you couldn't imagine. An old legend reads that the day a female neon graces our world, the bridge between us and the Temulus will forever be connected through her harmony. You see, the power of a flower, a rose, has always been the way it can grow in the most unorthodox of places. A rose cannot live for long if plucked, so it has thorns to protect itself. A Neon is that rose. Slowly peeling off each petal and revealing a power so great that not even a god can touch." Ford paused for a few long seconds.

"Penelope...I know you're a virgin." Ford gazed at me.

"What! No. No, I'm not! That's crazy! Why would you even say that?!" I panicked.

79

"I could tell. The way I projected my thoughts. You were nervous. You were wanting. I could feel your heat."

I started sweating. He was making me a little too hot. "Oh, um, okay! That was random. You think I'm this power yielding goddess that's going to defeat this ruby magic and bring these worlds together?" I started to laugh. Ford looked at me with a serious tone.

"Oh, my God. You really *do* think that. Seriously? What the hell, Ford! That is *not* me. I can't do that. I can't even remember the last time I was able to walk from one end of campus to the other without tripping over my own feet." I was nervously smiling.

"Look, Penelope, I want to help you. I want to help you harness your power."

A flash of Malee came to my mind. "Yeah, sure. Just like you helped Malee? Ha." I was still a little jealous. I didn't want to seem jealous.

"Penelope, look...you're my responsibility now." Ford looked down at his hands. "I wouldn't be able to sleep if I knew something had happened to you. Please, let me help you."

It took me a minute to begin processing everything I had just heard. Ford has saved my life twice already and there were unexplainable things happening. I had to do something.

"Penelope, let me introduce you to someone..."

I started to get up out of the bed. Ford led me out of the room. When I stepped into the hallway I was filled with intense emotion. The halls were a strong coffee color with ancient statues lining the walls on top of pillars like ancient Egyptian images I had seen. The markings on the ceiling were out of my league, but seemed to light up whenever I walked under them. Ford smiled and kept leading me through different hallways. We came to a long running corridor with large windows. The windows faced the outside of the castle. I could see tall trees, a beautiful forest, and colorful birds flying throughout the sky. What a beautiful sight. I watched the bright white clouds run through the sky. I kept looking out the window - I felt drawn to something out there. Suddenly, a huge animal flew right by me, growling and letting out an ear-piercing howl. I was startled, afraid, and fell back - Ford caught me. What the hell was that? It looked like a mix between a dragon and an eagle. It had the talons, the tail, and the body of a dragon, but its head and wings looked just like a beautiful eagle. It was a fluorescent green with a hue of blue. I was stunned. I couldn't speak, but I felt like it spoke to me.

"Ford, what was that? Where did it come from?" I was a nervous wreck.

"He's a Brindle. The only remaining one of his kind. He roams around our castle, but has no owner. That's the first time I've seen him since...the grand war." Ford looked out the window.

"The grand war? What grand war? Ford, you're still not telling me everything are you?" I was unsettled.

"I've told you almost everything, Penelope. Three hundred years ago the Neons turned to a tumultuous war with the Temulus after Danita was killed. We lost. We lost hundreds of our own people and our animals. We had dragons, eagles, every animal you could think of that could fly. They were all lost to the Temulus. They rule them and own them now. That Brindle you saw, his name is Creed. He fought with us those years ago, but never returned until now..." Ford looked at me with longing in his eyes. "Come."

I followed him down the long corridor to two solid vaulted doors. They were covered in gold. He opened them and we entered a large throne room. Ford motioned me to walk forward.

"Dad, Mom...this is Penelope."

Dad? Mom? What was he thinking? He could've at least told me he was going to introduce me to his parents. What the hell was I going to say? I was completely flabbergasted. I froze in my steps waiting for them to turn their chairs around. In that moment, the two thrones facing the enormous window turned to face us. Ford held my hand. I looked down and our hands were glowing. Mine pink, his green. My energy began to overpower his and I quickly let go.

Ford's mother was the most beautiful creature I had ever seen. She had light green skin with light hazel eyes that glittered when she blinked. Her dress was breathtaking. It was long and flowed down around her throne. She spoke in a relaxing tone. "Hi, Penelope, my name is Ruler Mara. I lead our Neon world."

Ford's father was a little odd-looking in the sense that he looked just like my father. That is to say, normal. There was nothing about him that suggested power, or warlock, or energy, or anything. Was this right? "Penelope, our son has told us much about you. I'm so glad we have finally met you. My name is Winsten. Ford says you're a Neon."

I looked at him uncomfortably. "I suppose I am. I didn't know I was, but Ford has shown me otherwise." Winsten looked at me and then at Ford with a questioning look.

"I didn't do anything. I didn't touch her!" Ford exclaimed in an undeserving pierced tone.

What did he mean? Didn't touch me? Of course he didn't. I was missing something, obviously. Then I thought about Malee...

I turned to Winsten and Mara. I closed my eyes and began thinking about my dad, my mom, and my two best friends. My hands began to glow pink and there was a pink circle of energy around my heart. I opened my eyes and could see the light emanating around me. I spooked myself and let go of my thoughts. The pink dissipated, but Winsten and Mara stood there looking at me in awe, Winsten's hands glowing green seemingly blocking Mara's power. What were those looks for? How did Winsten have green energy? "Ford, your job from here on out is to protect her. Don't let her out of your sight. The Temulus cannot know what she is." Mara ordered.

What I am? Yeah, it was a mystery to me as well.

"I think it's a little too late for that, Mother. I caught two of them from the Temulus world trying to capture her..." Ford looked at me with a worried and shielding demeanor.

"Ford, take her home. Help her understand, quickly. She cannot stay like this without control of what she has." Winsten led us through the vaulted doors.

This was all so confusing, but I had ONE burning question. The doors closed behind us and we stood in the long corridor. "Ford!" I spoke quietly yet forcefully, "I will not do anything until you answer my question." Ford looked at me with worry.

"How did Malee get her powers? I'm not leaving this corridor until you tell me."

Ford walked slowly to me and pushed his body onto mine. He held my face in the palm of his hands, running his fingers through the ends of my hair. "Your hair is beautiful. I've never seen such dark, shimmering, coffee colored hair. It's entrancing." I grabbed his hand and pulled it down to his side.

"Tell me." I demanded.

Ford grabbed my hand and we were immediately transported back to his house in the woods.

"Wait, before you tell me. You said you can only teleport someone if they are strong enough. Does that mean I am strong and, if so, who else have you been able to do that with?" I was curious. Ford took a deep breath.

"Yes, that means you are strong Penelope. But you knew that. And you are the only one I've been able to transport. Are you satisfied?"

I nodded with relief and smiled. "Okay, now onto my question."

"Penelope. I want to be honest with you, so please don't take it for more than what it is."

I looked at him and nodded. He kept explaining...

"Well, I told you Malee and I were together before. I met her one day when she worked at a place next door to The Port. She was a waitress at one of the restaurants. Some guys were picking on her out back while she was throwing out the trash, and I came to her rescue."

"Hmm, seems like you do that often." I snarled.

"Penelope..." Ford paused.

"It's fine go on."

"I rescued her and showed her The Port. We hung out with each other mostly during the day. It took her a while to find out I was a Neon. She wasn't afraid and refused to leave my side when I told her it was too dangerous. Eventually, we became serious and became intimate. She and I decided to have sex one night." Ford stopped and put his hand to his forehead. I tried to contain my jealousy.

"Ford, it's fine. I can handle it." I gulped.

"Penelope, we were kissing and rubbing our bodies against each other. Each time, I could see my energy pulsing through the parts of her I was touching. I didn't pay any mind and kept kissing her. It was getting more intense and I could see her eyes glowing green, so I stopped. She begged me to keep going. So, I took a condom out of my pocket, put it on, and put myself in between her...inside of her. At first, she started to moan, and I began feeling increasingly dominant. But as my dominance took hold, she began to gasp for air. My green energy was pulsing through her veins and out of her mouth and eyes. I stopped, but she kept gasping and had a green aura coming out of her. I didn't know what to do, so I brought her home. My mother's maidens looked after her and made her better. Penelope, she had absorbed some of my electric charges. Luckily, that's all that happened. I could've killed her. If we would've of kept on..."

I had heard enough. I was filled with jealousy at the details, but also compassion for Ford. He was upset.

"I changed Malee's life forever, and her course in this world. Now she has this green energy that she can't fully control, and sometimes it puts her in danger. That's my fault, I did that. I will never do that again. When I am intimate with women, my energy turns into dominance and it's hard for me to stay in control. When a Neon has sex with someone who is not of our world, we transfer some of our power to them and that power can ultimately kill them."

I paused and looked at his eyes. "Is that why Danita was your partner? Was she able to handle your...dominance?"

Ford looked at me in dismay. "Danita and I didn't have the chance to get so close. You didn't let me finish before, but she was killed before any of it could happen."

I looked down at my feet "I'm sorry, Ford."

"Penelope, I wasn't always a powerful Neon. I've felt the intimacy of women, I've slept with them."

I looked at Ford annoyed and with a raised eyebrow.

"The reason I'm telling you this is because, in the beginning, I refused my power. I refused to control it and I would suppress it continuously. My energy was the most powerful they had seen. My mother and father spent a lifetime helping me control it. But they couldn't control my passion, my emotions, my dominance."

I couldn't help but be attracted to Ford. His eyes were domineering, the way he took off his jacket, his muscular body. I walked over to him and put my hands on his chest. He closed his eyes and lowered his head. I could feel his rhythmic breathing. I reached up and touched my nose to his chin and then kissed him, my lips wrapping around his, and my breath becoming his breath. He shoved his tongue in my mouth and kissed me deeply. The sweet taste of his lips sucked me into a captivating trance. He grabbed my hips, yanking me close into his body, against his groin. I could feel him and I was turning him on. A green light began to glow between our lips, and he immediately pushed me away.

Chapter 6 - Desire's Block

"Penelope, I can't, we can't. I already told you what could happen." Ford took a step back.

I looked at him with embarrassment and disappointment. Ford was rejecting me. I quickly grabbed my jacket and stood up to leave.

"Penelope, wait, where are you going?"

"Ford, I don't think I can take your rejection. All of this, what we're going through. What I feel when I'm around you. I have to go." I ran to the front door of his house and opened it. I turned to look at Ford. "I have to figure this out on my own. I can't do it with you hovering over me!"

"Penelope, please, don't go. I'll do anything."

"Then kiss me." I demanded.

Ford hesitated.

"You see. You can't even do that. How am I supposed to harness my desire if the one person that I desire won't even help me!" There, I had said it. Out loud. I couldn't get Ford out of my head. I desired him. He stood there looking at me with his fierce green-lit eyes. He hadn't heard me say those words directly, but I know he knew. Ever since he had gotten into my mind, I couldn't get him out.

Ford walked over to me and shut the door behind me. His eyes locked on mine, his lips pursed in my direction. "Penelope, not only am I able to destroy you if we get too close, but you're a virgin. It could take a long time for you to discover your sexuality, and what you like in order to fully harness your power. I don't want to get in the way of that."

What did he mean 'get in the way'?

"Trust me, Penelope." He took my hand and transported me back to campus. I saw Lyla and Ronnie in the distance. They seemed to be enjoying the sun and some conversation by some trees.

"Pen! Where have you been? We've been waiting for you! What happened after breakfast?" Lyla was anxious. "I saw you with Ford just now. Where did he go?" Lyla looked over in the distance

I looked around and realized Ford was gone. Ronnie looked at me with an impatient face. I could tell he was concerned and maybe, just maybe, a little jealous. I had no words, only thoughts. I couldn't begin to tell them both what had happened. I don't know if I even wanted to. The only person that would really understand was Malee and, as luck would have it, I saw Malee and Sarina walking towards us.

"So, how did it go with Ford? Anything interesting come up?" Malee rolled her eyes.

"Nothing, really. He just wanted to know I was okay coming back to campus and everything. You know, after what happened at The Port." I nonchalantly answered.

"Yeah, I bet he really wanted to take care of you." Malee spoke in an offhand tone.

"I have to go." I responded.

Ronnie and Lyla seemed to sense the tension.

"Yeah, I have to go check on some stuff in the library." Ronnie responded.

"Hmm, same. Well, except maybe not in the library." Lyla laughed.

I quietly walked back to my dorm and opened the door. Velaire was there. Doing her make-up and listening to some music on her headphones. As I stepped in she pulled off her headset. "Pen! Can I call you Pen?" I nodded. "So glad you're here! So, you need to hurry up and get ready. Tonight, there is a massive party and we are going!"

I gave her a look of doubt "Vel, I don't know...I'm not sure I'm up for it." I sat on my bed and pulled out my laptop.

"Oh, come on Pen! Just think about it! You'll get to have fun, meet new people! Most of them looking to have a good time!" She winked. Little did she know I hadn't ever "partied" like that.

Hmm, maybe that is what I needed. I needed to forget about Ford rejecting me, about this grand war, and...my power. These were ridiculous things someone trying to gear up for med school should not have to worry about. Sure, my friends and I had had waited a couple of years and taken community college classes to improve our admissions to Duke, but I was still new to the scene. I had taken a break between high school and college to explore my interests. I lay in bed and listened to Imogen Heap and about another hour later I sat up.

"Vel, fine, I will go."

She threw her hands up and let out a squeal. "Yay, Pen! Let's do it! Okay, so this party tonight. It's a masquerade/ supernatural theme."

"What? Vel, no. I don't have anything like that in my closet." I mean, I did have this little ability to harness powerful energy. But of course, she didn't need to know that...I guess I was cut out for this party. Why not? I grabbed a black silk dress from my closet and headed to the art building. Surely they would have some interesting items I could use to make myself a mask. "I'll meet you back here in an hour Vel."

I got to the art building and walked down a long hallway to a craft room they had designed as "open creativity." I walked in and saw the walls were lined with all kinds of markers, pencils, crayons, stencils, ribbon, paper, everything you could think of. I grabbed some cardboard and got to work. About 45 minutes had gone by. Okay, it was getting late. I had better head out to meet Vel before she took off without me. I hated going to parties alone. Surely, Ronnie and Lyla were invited. As I walked out of the craft room and into the hallway, I saw a blue light protruding from underneath one of the doors. It was the same blue light from The Port. Oh, no...but this time, I was armed with more information and more control. I walked towards the door and could feel the energy behind it grow. It's almost as if the closer I got the more it was disturbed. I got to the door and put my hand on the doorknob. My hands began to glow. I pulled the door open and stood in the doorway ready to face what was on the other side. My eyes narrowed, my legs planted, and my arms bulged at my sides with pink energy. I looked across the room and could see a small, white, cylinder-like object floating in the middle of the room. It was surrounded by blue electric charges and pulsing with every step I took towards it. What was it?

Before I could take any more steps, I heard a voice in my head. Of course. "Penelope, it's a blue orb-sphere created by Sirens as a trap. Next to ruby magic, to have the power of that orb-sphere would mean to hold the power of a thousands suns. If you touch that right now, it will kill you. When it senses danger, it explodes."

Ugh, get out of my head! I pushed Ford out of my mind.

Was that the blast of blue light I was hit with at The Port? Why was this orb-sphere presenting itself to me? It hadn't exploded when I opened the door, or when I stepped close, like the other one. I heard a voice down the hallway.

"Pen!" I heard Lyla.

I quickly stepped back and the orb-sphere vanished into thin air.

"Velaire told me you might be down here! Figured I would come and get you so we could walk to the party to-gether? Ronnie is outside."

"Yeah, Lyla, hey. I was just down here trying to get some stuff together for this party. Yeah, let's go." I walked over to Lyla a little disoriented, but well enough to pick up the pace as we made our way out of the art building.

Sure enough, there was Ronnie.

"Hey Penelope, you ready for this?" Ronnie took my arm, then Lyla's and we walked towards the dorm to meet up with Velaire. The three of us walked towards one of the frat houses a few blocks down on campus. The music was loud, everyone was dressed up, and people were screaming, and everyone was having a good time. We knocked on the door and Sarina opened it. What a surprise. I'm sure Malee was going to be here, too.

"Hi, come on in," The inside of the house was adorned with kegs, a ping pong table, a pool table, and an actual pool, in the backyard. Velaire strolled off to converse with some friends. Ronnie, Lyla, and me decided to walk over to the kitchen and get some snacks.

"Pen, are you okay? Has everything been okay so far? I'm worried about you." Ronnie was concerned, but thoughtful. "I keep seeing you with Ford, and ever since the whole Port incident, I just don't trust the guy." Ronnie poured himself a drink. I looked at him with disappointment. Disappointment in myself. I hadn't been a good friend to him and Lyla the last few days--the most important time as we started this new chapter in our lives. I grabbed a cup and asked Ronnie to pour me some beer. "Pen, are you sure? You want a drink?"

"Sure, what the hell! I've got the rest of my life to get it all right." Or so I thought. I could hear him in my mind. *"Penelope, be careful drinking. Too much will impair your judgment and your power will be difficult to control. Please, don't do anything you'll regret."*

I was furious! Was he still stalking me? Pretty sure one beer wasn't going to completely alter my senses. I wanted to block him out of my head...for good. But how could I do that? I should be able to, right? If I'm as powerful as he thinks I am, then I should be able to block him out of my mind.

"Penelope." In that moment, I turned to see the redheaded, busty girl looking at me.

"Sarina." I gulped. There was something about her. Something alluring. I couldn't understand what it was, and I sure as hell didn't want to know. She was Malee's friend, and I had done enough damage there. She handed me a drink.

"Here you go. Want to try something a little stronger than this keg beer that tastes like filth?" I mean, what did she expect? Did she want some top of the line beer on tap on a college kid's budget? I looked at her with hesitation and glanced around the room. So many people drinking and laughing. I felt like I didn't belong.

"No, thank you. I'll stick with my beer."

"Suit yourself." She gently responded.

I was about to walk the other way when she took my arm. "Penelope. I know what you are." She looked me dead in my eyes. I gasped. How could she know? Did Malee say something to her? In my heightened sense, I pulled my arm away and stared at her in shock.

"Tell me, how do you keep both of these power from killing you?" She smiled at me. She moved in closer and whispered in my ear, "Penelope, I can help you harness what Ford won't."

A nervous laugh came over me. "Sarina, I don't know what you're talking about. Frankly, I'm not interested in harnessing anything. I'm not what anyone thinks I am, especially Ford."

I started walking backwards in the direction of the stairs. Maybe if I could just sneak away and ignore she ever said that to me then all would be well. Sarina kept her eyes locked on mine. Her dangerous eyes pierced through my mind. What was happening? I felt a sudden urge, a feeling, a good feeling, run through my veins down between my legs. Okay, no, this could not be possible. She had to be some kind of Neon or power wielder. She could probably make people want her. I'm betting that's what she was trying to do. I heard his voice again...

"Penelope...Sarina, is one of us...she's a Neon. If you're wondering what she's thinking try touching her hand to see if you can read her mind. I knew another Neon was here I just didn't know who."

It took all my might and what I had learned about meditation to completely block Ford out. I counted to three...1...2...3...I couldn't hear him anymore, or feel him. Oh, thank God!

Sarina was still looking at me. Touch her hand? I mean, she was another Neon but what would I say? Can I please hold your hand? How awkward would that be? I looked at her and asked her to sit next to me on the couch. As we sat down I grabbed her hand and focused all my energy on reading her thoughts. She felt powerfully emotional and full of desire.

Sarina took my hips and pulled them close to her. She began kissing my neck and gripped the straps of my black dress with her teeth. What was happening? I moaned with gratitude as she slid her hands over my breasts. She massaged them and licked down my neck. My breathing was fast. It was all happening so quickly. She pulled my dress down from my right shoulder exposing my breast. Her mouth covered my hard nipple and she began to tongue around it. Her tongue slid up my neck and to my lips. She was kissing me deeply with her tongue in every part of my mouth. As her hand slowly moved onto my inner-thigh and up my dress, she whispered in my ear, "Penelope."

I quickly let go of her hand. Oh God! What had just happened? Holy hell. I had just read her desires. She wanted me. As I breathed heavily I couldn't help but stare at her with no words coming out of my mouth. She stared me straight in the eyes.

Out of breath, I ran out of the living room, and out of the house. I fell to my knees filled with anxiety. What the hell was that? How did I do that? Is that really what Sarina was thinking? I don't understand. Why did I like it? I had so many questions. I looked up and standing in front of me was Ford. Seriously? Was this how my night was going to end? He helped me up.

"Penelope."

"Ford, just stop. I don't feel like it tonight."

He walked by my side as I headed back to my dorm room. I let him inside after I readied myself for bed.

"Okay, fine. How did you know what I was thinking?"

"I could feel you Penelope. I felt your reservation and I could feel who was around you. Especially Sarina." He smirked.

"Okay. Sarina, what was all that about? I did what you said. I held her hand to read her mind and all of a sudden, I was part of this sexual fantasy. She was all over me...and...I liked it. I think." I took a deep breath and stared at Ford, waiting for an answer.

"When you touched her hand she projected her thoughts into your mind. Except, why would she have those thoughts about you? Unless, she was trying to help you with the power she knows you have. Only my parents, you, and me know about you. That can't be. I need to find out what Sarina knows." Ford took a breath and was about to leave my room.

I grabbed his arm and pulled him towards me. "Can you stay? Please? At least until I'm asleep?"

Ford looked at me with a smile. "I thought you didn't want me around. You blocked me out of your head..."

"Wait, how did you know that?"

"I told you, Penelope. I can feel you, all of you..."

His words were daggers to my core. I swallowed loudly.

"Ford, you said I was strong. How do I know how strong I am when I can't even test it against another great power?" I pulled his arm closer towards my bed. I sat down. " According to your parents, you are supposed to protect me and help me, but I guess they may not know I am having trouble harnessing one tiny pillar. Desire." I pulled his arm further until he was sitting on my bed.

"Penelope. I already told you, I won't. Part of protecting you means..."

I moved in close and put my hand to his lips. "Can you at least show me again? What you showed me at Malee's apartment?"

Ford looked at me with a smile and took my hand. My mind was transported. *We were in a log cabin. A loud fire was roaring and crackling. Ford, holding my hand, led me to a plush rug on the floor in front of the fireplace. I was wearing my tight black dress and he had on a black shirt with light-colored jeans. His biceps protruded from his sleeves. He sat me down and began to kiss my lips. He was gentle but strong.and his need to overpower me moved to my cheek, and slowly down my neck. I shivered.*

This was too much for me. I couldn't take not being a part of his world, being apart from him. I let go of his hand and we were back in my dorm room.

"Ford, please. We don't have to have sex. We can do other things so you can help me with my desire. I need to know how powerful I can be."

Ford looked at me with hesitation. "Penelope, even if I help you, you saw what happened with Sarina. It's not just me that can unlock your desire. Just like Xela, the pillar of desire, you have to experiment. You have to find out."

"Fine, then I want to find out first with you. I don't care about Sarina. I'm not scared. I can handle what you're afraid of."

I pulled him in close. I could feel his breath on my lips. His hands were interlocked with mine. His body close enough I could smell his pheromones. God, he smelled so good.

"Penelope..." I heard his voice tremble as I took his hand and placed it around my waist. He moved in closer and began kissing me, passionately. His lips tasted sweet and I could feel his stubble around his chin. It was sexy. He moved from my lips down to my chin, and slowly down my neck. I pulled away for a second and looked down at my hands. No pink energy...

"Penelope. Your power won't come out this way. I know how to draw it out of you. I know what you like...what you need."

How could he know if I didn't even know?

"Show me." I replied softly.

"I will, but not here." He reached for my hand and transported us to his house. Except, this time, we were in his bedroom. His fireplace was roaring. It was warm. He carried me and placed me on the bed. "Wait here." He said anxiously.

I watched him walk over to his closet. His closet was bigger than my dorm room! From his dresser, he grabbed what seemed like rope ties. Okay, what the hell was going on? He walked back over to the bed.

"Um, yeah, not sure if that's going to fit what I was thinking," I said doubtfully.

Sensing my hesitation, Ford said, "Penelope, you trust me don't you?" His voice was deep. Sexy.

"Yes, I do."

He walked over to me and began to kiss me. " I kissed you the last time so I could show you your power, but you didn't respond to some of my cues. It wasn't until I forcefully pulled your head back by your hair that you displayed some kind of sexual desire."

I gulped loudly. Maybe he did know something I didn't.

Chapter 7 – Flower

"Penelope. If you want me to do this, you will have to trust me. Trust me with your mind, your body." Him saying those words sent chills down my spine. My heart was warm and the sensation was all over me.

"I do, Ford. I trust you."

"Good. There is only one thing you need to remember. If at any point you want me to stop what I'm doing, just say the word, ruby." Ford unwound the rope ties.

I took another deep breath. I wasn't sure about what he was going to do, but I had never tried it like this. I had only ever kissed someone before, let alone let them do whatever they wanted to my body. But this was what I asked for. I wanted him...

"Why ruby?" I asked.

"Because, with the evil word ruby, there will be no mistake you want me to stop. I have to be careful, I have to give myself limits...if my dominance takes hold..."

"Ford. Stop. I can handle it..." I reassured him. I sat up and looked in his eyes. He was focused on me, completely. He took the rope ties and walked over to the bed. He placed them next to me and leaned in to kiss me. His hands running through my hair, entangling them. With a sudden tug, he pulled my head back exposing my neck. He put his nose to my neck and took in my scent.

"Penelope. I've wanted you ever since I felt your energy at The Port."

My breathing was faster. My heart was racing. He looked like the sexy Neon I saw full of rage at The Port. His hand still entangled in my hair, he began to kiss me underneath my chin, slowly circling my neck with his tongue, holding my head back. I couldn't move it. I liked it.

He whispered in my ear. "Penelope. I can't expect you to tell me what you like, so we'll play it by ear... " I smiled and moved my head so my ear would rub against his lips.

Ford started to raise my silk shirt. I was in my sleep-wear. He raised it over my head and threw it across the room. I didn't have a bra. He looked down at my breasts and bit his lip just staring for a few seconds. Green shining through his eyes. "You're so perfect." He continued. He leaned forward and to kiss my breasts. His left hand reached up to pull my hair. I tipped my head back. He placed his tongue and gently made circles around my now erect nipple. He began to suck on it and engulf his mouth with everything I had to offer. My hands were a dim pink and I felt the pleasure through my body. He held my breast in place as he sucked on my nipple and pushed his entire body against me. I began to groan. My hands still a dim pink.

Ford ripped his shirt off and hovered over me, his biceps bulging. His body was entrancing. His abs delightfully de-fined. He ran his hand up my thigh and the side of my body. With each touch, there was green pulsing through my body. He held his breath for a second and I looked in his eyes. I was longing for him. I didn't want him to stop. I grabbed his hand and put it back on my thigh. He leaned in to kiss me and dug his tongue deep into my mouth. He was a little more intense this time. Running his hand up my stomach and again to my breast...placing my nipple in between his thumb and index finger. He toyed with it; he played, and then forcefully pinched it. I yelped and quickly sat up. My hands were glowing with pink energy. I looked at them in amazement, and then I looked at Ford. My breathing was heavy.

I threw myself at him and he pushed me against the bed. He yanked off my silk shorts and began to kiss my thighs. "Penelope." He continued to kiss me up my thigh. He got to my bellybutton and traced it with his tongue. I couldn't control my breathing. My eyes were closed as I moaned loudly.

"Shhhh, Penelope. Try to control your breathing." He reached up and briefly cupped his hand over my mouth as he kissed me below my navel, my hips moving rhythmically in circles.

With my breasts exposed and hands loose, I reached down to feel his hair. He grabbed the rope and took both of my arms. Pulling my arms behind my back he began to tie my hands together. His green energy shining through his hands and my pink energy mirroring the charge. The more intense his power came, the more mine matched it. He tied my hands as tight as they could be without hurting me. When he was done, he whispered in my ear "Penelope. Remember the word I told you." I nodded. His body and all of his weight was on me...I couldn't move. His hand slid down to the top of my mound. He kissed me ferociously as he put his fingers above my sex. My moaning was getting longer and high-pitched. I tried to wriggle from underneath him, but he was strong. I wanted to meet his every touch, every inch of his body lining up with mine. I was in another world. This feeling. I would have never believed I would be with someone like him. He was the one I had been waiting for...wise but also strong, sexy, and he smelled intoxicating.

With his hand over my sex, he moved two fingers over my clitoris and I gasped. It felt so good and my body was responding eagerly. I was dripping with intensity and my nipples were erect longing for his warm touch. I wanted his fingers inside of me to make me scream with pleasure. I wanted him so much. My hands were still pink with energy, and as I looked down at what he was doing, I could see his green energy run rampant throughout my sex. He saw it too. He didn't stop and kept drawing small motions with his fingers. His lips locked on mine, taking me in. And me...I was taking him in. His hand was so warm and soft. As he continued massaging my clitoris in sensual circles, his mouth sucked and tugged at my nipples. My wetness was pouring out of me and my breathing was in tempo with his muscular chest. I arched my body in pleasure, unrestrained.

I felt as if I was going to explode.

He whispered in my ear, "Penelope, I'm not going to go inside of you until you're ready. Ready for me. But right now, I want you to come for me." His two fingers now circled faster. My insides were on fire and I couldn't hold it in anymore. I exploded and released all the tension I had been feeling the last few days. A bright pink light shot out of my mouth as I tilted my head back. I yelled his name "Oh, Ford!" He hovered his hand over my mouth to cover the energy from destroying what was in its path. His green electric pulse neutralizing mine.

"Penelope. I want to be the first and last person you do this with. Any of this. This is the desire you need to learn to control...with me." My body convulsed and I shivered. I hadn't felt this before. Let alone seen a huge pink ray of light shoot out of me! Ford was still on me. I could feel his erection. He ran his fingers along my wetness and then licked them. "You taste good." I smiled at him. He was erotic, this was erotic. He reached behind me to untie my hands. His aura of green energy subsided and his green-lit eyes turned a dull color. He climbed into bed and pulled me next to him. He knew my desires..."Ford..." I nuzzled his neck and fell asleep.

I awoke after a few hours and it was still dark outside. I looked over, but Ford wasn't in bed. I grabbed my phone and had several missed calls from Vel, Ronnie, and Lyla. Great, they were probably worried after I had scurried out of the frat house. Sarina hitting on me wasn't exactly what I was expecting when I decided to have a fun night out. I grabbed a robe hanging on a rack beside the bed and walked out to the living room. Ford was sitting by the fireplace, no shirt and wearing a pair of jeans, talking on the phone. Who was he talking to at almost 3am? I could hear him yelling at someone as I walked in. He turned to look at me and his eyes were bright green. He was huffing and still holding the phone to his ear.

"Ford, what's the matter? What's wrong?" I ran over to him.

"There's been an attack. The Temulus. They went after Malee tonight."

"What!" I exclaimed. "When? Where? Where is she now?"

"She's at her apartment. I have to go there now. I also need to find out how Sarina knew about you."

A little spark of jealousy stirred within me. I didn't want him to go. If she was at her apartment then she was okay. "Is someone with her?" I asked.

"Yes, her mother. And maybe Sarina." Ford furrowed his eyebrows. "I don't want you anywhere around Sarina or her little games. Don't let her touch you again." He quickly walked over to me and took my face in his hands. He kissed me with fervor and pulled me close. "Listen. Penelope. I have to go there, I should probably take you back to your dorm. Your friends will be worried in the morning."

Ford led us to his armored truck. I was still feeling a little heated and jealous on the ride back to the dorm. I didn't want Ford to be with Malee. Especially after everything he had told me, and how she got her powers. And he was going to be around some power-yielding temptress? I was quiet. When we arrived to campus I quickly got out of the car.

"Thanks...hope Malee is okay, or whatever." I turned away to walk in the door.

"Penelope, wait. You know I can't just leave her like that. She was attacked tonight. That probably wouldn't have happened if it weren't for me..."

"Yeah, sure. Fine. I get it." I kept walking.

"Penelope..." Ford stood next to his truck facing me.

"Shouldn't you be hurrying up to make sure she's okay? Bye Ford!" I walked in the door.

When I got to my room, I slowly opened the door. Velaire was fast asleep. I climbed into bed and laid thinking about the events that had transpired. I couldn't stop thinking about Ford and how he had made me feel. I wanted more. I wanted more of him. I kept thinking about him and what he could be doing at Malee's apartment. It was already 4:30am and I had not slept a wink. I managed to get a couple of hours in before Velaire jumped on top of my bed.

"Penelope! Oh my God! You're okay! Where did you go? We were worried sick!"

I barely had both eyes open. I just wanted to sleep. I threw the pillow over my head. "I'm fine. I just ended up talking to Ford all night and walking around campus."

"What! With Ford? Ha. That's interesting. Seems like a questionable guy from what I've heard." Vel chuckled.

"What do you mean from what you've heard?" I demanded.

"Well, Malee said some things about him last night. You know, how he likes to play games and be with different women, you know..."

Of course Malee had said that!

"You know what, Vel, I gotta go!" I shook my head.

"Was it something I said? Pen! Come back!" I could hear Vel yell. I rushed down to my car and headed towards Malee's apartment. I couldn't stand the thought of him being there, and with Sarina!

I quickly drove to get there, and when I arrived, the door was unlocked and I let myself in. "Ford? Malee?...Sarina?" No response. As I slowly walked towards the end of the apartment I heard noises of a struggle. I ran towards the back room and was about to open the door when I heard Ford's voice.

"Sarina! Tell me what you know! Now."

I pushed the door open and Malee was lying in bed with a cast around her arm and leg, and a terrified look on her face. "Ford, don't! Sarina didn't know about anything! She was just messing with Penelope! I told her to do it!" She had.

I looked over at Ford and he had Sarina pushed up against the wall with his hand around her neck, a green pulse circling around it. She was gasping for air. I could see her hands begin to glow a dull green.

"Ford, no! Let her go! Don't do this!" I yelled at him.

"Penelope. What are you doing here?" Ford let go of his grip and Sarina fell to the ground. He stood back and positioned himself in front of me. Sarina ran out of the bedroom and out of the house.

"Ford, what the hell is your problem?" I demanded. "You could've killed her! She's a Neon. She's one of you!"

"She may be one of us, but after what she tried to pull with you! She'd better stay away from you and me." Ford's breathing was still heavy. He turned to look at Malee.

"From you and her?" Malee was upset."What do you mean you and her? Are you two like a thing now? Were you going to just take someone like her and turn her into someone like me? Oh, well, I guess you can have whatever girl you want Ford! I survived. So now you think someone like her can? She won't!" Malee grew more emotional.

"Malee, it's not like that. Penelope. Well...she needs my help." Ford tried to soothe her.

Wait, what? I need his help? This was his chance to tell her that at some point now, or in the near future, we would stay in each other's lives much like they had been. I could feel my heart burn and a hint of anxiety crept up my throat.

"I need your help? That's all you have to say? Your help huh?" Totally furious, I turned to walk out the door.

Ford stopped me in the hallway. "Penelope! Wait! Malee was attacked. Now is not the right time."

"Oh really. Not the right time? Yeah, well, last night was not the right time either I suppose?"

"I didn't say that." Ford looked at me. He gave me a look of disappointment.

"And I guess saving me at the Port, or the book store, wasn't the *right time* either." I retorted.

"Penelope. Please."

I shoved my hand away from Ford. "Go tend to Malee. She needs you." I continued walking out of the house.

I slammed the door and got into my car. A tear rolled down my face. How could he not say anything about the two of us to Malee? It was her right to know and his responsibility to tell her. I started my car and drove back to campus. On the way back I spotted Sarina walking inside an old building right near the bookstore. She was carrying a black duffel bag. What was she doing? Was she catching up on some summer art? Yeah, right. I wanted to know what she knew, what Ford was trying to get out of her. I parked my car and quickly ran towards the building. I slowly opened the side door and slid inside. I was at the top of a staircase. As I stealthily descended, the building was dark and at the bottom I came to what looked like an old theater performance studio. There was a large stage with props and a backdrop. Wooden pillars and planks were strewn all over the floor. There were some lights on, and I could hear some rustling on the stage. I tried to stay hidden amongst the chairs. I ducked in between a couch and a chair. I could see Sarina walk onto the stage. She took her duffel bag and pulled out a cylindrical item wrapped in a thick cloth. I watched with intent as she began unraveling it. Slowly, I began to see a blue light emanate from underneath the cloth. What the heck was that? Then I realized she had an orb-sphere.

She stood in front of it as it floated in the middle of the stage. I could see her begin to glow. Her eyes were green and her hands were surrounded by a green charge. How did she have an orb-sphere? Where did she get it? If she knows what an orb-sphere is, then she must know more than Ford thinks. Wait, was she glowing green?

Sarina reached up with her hands and began to move them towards the orb-sphere's aura. Did she know what it would do to her if she touched it? Surely not. Or did she? There's no way she would survive it. What was she trying to do? As she placed her hands around the orb-sphere, her green energy began to connect with the blue light. Her arms suddenly turned a bright green and her eyes and mouth shot out with an intense charge. Before I could yell out, I could see the orb-sphere sucking the life out of her. It was draining the color from her face, and her body began to convulse.

"Sarina!" I ran towards her and leaped on the stage. I channeled the pink energy from my hands, Ford's encounter still fresh on my mind. I reached out to grab Sarina's hands. I pulled her away from the charge and blocked the orb-sphere's energy with my pulses. Sarina fell to the ground. Within a second the orb-sphere vanished.

"Sarina! Are you okay?" I frantically asked and raised her head into my lap. She was still glowing green and her eyes were bright. She looked up at me.

"Thank you, Penelope." She closed her eyes.

As soon as the orb-sphere vanished I heard loud crashing noises coming from behind the stage. I turned around and I could see creatures in black cloaks. Oh no...they were the same ones I had encountered outside the stadium that night. Were they Temulus? How were there so many? Four, five, six! Where did they come from? I looked down at Sarina.

"Sarina!" I patted her cheek. "Sarina! We have to go!"

She opened her eyes and looked behind us. The two men in cloaks were dripping saliva from their mouths and blasting energy cycles all around the room. The stage was falling all around us and dust was flying all over.

"Penelope. I can't move. I'm too weak." Sarina whispered. "Penelope. The pillars. Use your power." She looked at me with helplessness.

How did she know I had power? That I could harness the four pillars of power? She did know about me! Ford was right. It wasn't time for questioning.

"Penelope." I heard one of them call out. "Twice now you have evaded your fate. But it is our luck that you have come this close." He licked his lips as saliva continued to drip down his face.

Another hissed. "Oh, and you brought a friend for us to play with. We are pretty hungry, but hadn't planned for it."

"Stay back. Unless part of your plan is to die!" I stood looking at them with my body ready to fight. I closed my eyes and began to think about my energy, my emotions, my mind, my desires. A circle of pink energy began emanating from around my body and my hands. I wasn't sure how else to release my power. Ford and I hadn't really explored how to send or shoot out electric pulses.

Sarina noticed my hesitation and spoke harshly. "Pen, when you feel your fingertips tingle, direct all of your energy out of them!"

I placed my hands in front of me in the direction of the Temulus. I shot out an electric charge. As soon as I hit one and he dissipated, the rest rushed towards me. Sarina gathered her might and began to fight the flying creatures alongside me on the stage. Two, three, four, five down. One more to go. Sarina and I looked at each other. We concentrated our power and shot a pulse towards the last remaining creature. He was right in front of us. The pink and green charge shot towards his black cloak and seemed to dissipate. Under his cloak I saw the tip of a wooden stick. It was glowing with green and pink charges as if it had absorbed our pulses. My eyes widened.

A talisman.

"I have a message for you." He towered over us. "Harness and do with your power what you will. But your rightful place will soon be discovered." And with one swish, he flew over us and vanished. I laid next to Sarina in shock, my energy spent. I knew we had to get out of here and move to safety.

Chapter 8 - The Red Affair

Carrying Sarina out of the theater basement took all the energy out of me, and as soon as we made it out the door, I stumbled and fell. The sky was darkening and I needed to get us both to safety. I wasn't sure how many of those *things* were out there. I put her arm around my shoulder and started to walk towards my car.

"Penelope!" Ford ran to help me. "What happened? I felt you were in trouble and I came to find you. Are you okay? What happened with Sarina?"

My shock had partially subsided and I began to spill everything to Ford.

"What? Penelope, we have to take her to my parent's. She can't heal like this. If she really tried to absorb the orb-sphere's power then she needs an antidote, and fast."

"How are you going to get her there if you can't transport her? She's too weak." I exclaimed. What are we going to do?" I questioned.

"I don't know! Let me think!" Ford answered.

Ford picked her up and hoisted her into his armored truck. I followed behind. He drove fiercely towards his house in the woods.

We parked outside his house and he held Sarina in his arms as we made our way through the tunnels. Finally, I could see the door. I ran to the door and saw a small black box with a red ribbon placed neatly in front of his door.

"Ford, what is it?" I asked as we both approached his door.

"I don't know. Don't pick it up." We walked inside and Ford laid Sarina on the couch.

Ford rushed to his bedroom and came back out with a black bag and headed to the kitchen. He put a small pot of water on the stove and took some leaves out of the bag. They were glowing. Ford lowered the leaves into a steeper he had placed in the pot of water. The white light faded and smoke fizzled out of the pot. He poured the antidote in a small cup and headed over to the couch where Sarina was laying. He sat her up and she began to slowly wake.

"Sarina. You need to drink this. If you touched the orb-sphere, you need rest, and you need to drink this."

She took the cup from Ford and drank its contents then lay back down. Ford walked to the closet to grab a blanket. I went to the front door for the box. I desperately wanted to know what it was.

"Penelope, don't!" Ford stopped my hand and held it against the box. "Don't. We don't know what is in it. Let me open it." Judging by what he had in his little black bag, and how Sarina carried around the orb-sphere, I handed the box to Ford and closed the door.

Ford started to untie the ribbon. I moved closer to look over his shoulder. He opened the box and inside was a single rose petal with a card. The rose petal was shiny and a beautiful red color. He took the card out and held it up for both of us to read.

"You have something that is not yours to keep. Only the truth can release her own potential." The card was signed, *Chez.*

Ford crushed the box with his bare hands. He flexed his arms and, with pure rage, let out a deep yell. His eyes lit up fiercely. He took the rose petal and the card, and threw them into the fireplace.

"Ford...Ford!" I tried to get his attention. He sat by the fireplace with his hands on his chin, thinking.

"Ford." I sat next to him.

"What was that all about? Who is Chez?" I looked at him with worry.

"Penelope. You aren't safe here. I need to take you somewhere where they can't hurt you. The Temulus found you because they were drawn to the power of the orb-sphere. They are also drawn to you because of your power. Us being together is like a beacon for them. I'm going to take you back to The Kingdom." Ford was pacing.

"Ford! Stop. Just stop for a minute. Well, at least I know your parent's enormous castle has a name." I tried to break his anger with sarcasm. "Okay, The Kingdom. Fine! But...who is...Chez? He...or she...was referring to me on that card weren't they?" I confirmed.

"He. And...yes. He knows what you are and that you're here. Which is why we can't stay here. I'm taking you to my parents. You'll be safer around other Neons that can help you. I'll stay with Sarina until she is better. Malee is fine. She took a beating, but she will be fine. The Temulus must have been after what Sarina had. Malee had told me she was hiding something powerful the last time we talked. I spent a lot of time with her to try and find out what it was. I didn't imagine it was an orb-sphere. Malee claims she was trying to keep it from getting in the wrong hands but, after what you told me about Sarina...I'm not sure she was on the same page. That power from the orb-sphere can take over you. Make you do things you shouldn't."

"Ford, let me help." I pleaded.

"No. Your powers are not strong enough yet."

"What? Sarina and I killed those Temulus in the theater!" I exclaimed.

"Yes, I know. But this. This is bigger than that. Just please." Ford took my hand and transported us to The Kingdom.

We started off in a field in front of the Kingdom. The trees were bright green and the same colorful birds were flying overhead. We walked up to the door and Ford let me inside. His parents were in the corridor.

"Mother. Father. Penelope needs to stay here. There have been some things happening. Malee, Sarina, and Penelope were attacked by Temulus Cloaks. They are all okay, but I'm not risking Penelope being out there."

Winsten looked at me and held out his hand. "Penelope, come." He ordered.

"We'll settle her in." Ford's mother assured him.

Ford smiled and vanished within seconds. I followed Winsten down the corridor, Mara close behind. Cloaks, so that's what they called them.

"I know Ford is protecting you, Penelope, but soon you will need to learn how to really protect yourself. Our son will soon need your help." Winsten kept talking.

What was he talking about? There was no way I was going to be this Goddess to bring their worlds together. I still couldn't wrap my head around that. I had so much to learn, so many questions, so little time. We walked past the floor to ceiling windows again. I stopped.

"Winsten, Mara. If it's all right, may I just sit for a minute? I need to gather my thoughts." I asked.

I sat down on the nearest couch and put my head in my hands.

"Abigail, bring that tea over here, the rest of the house can wait!" Mara called out towards the hall where a nicely dressed young woman was pushing a cart of tea. She rushed towards me and poured me a cup.

"Drink up, Penelope. When you're up for it, come to our quarters and we will show you to your room." Mara took Winsten's hand and led him away to the two gold doors. I felt a sense of comfort. Mara had a very nice voice and it was soothing. It helped me calm down after the chaos.

I walked over to the windows where I had seen the flying animal when I was here last. I couldn't remember its name but I felt something when it flew by me. I wanted to get outside. Maybe I could find it. I hurried down the corridor and found a door that led outside to the back of the castle. I let myself out and entered a garden filled with wildflowers. Green, blue, pink, red, almost every color of the rainbow. The flowers towered over the brick path I was standing on. There was fog in the distance, but I could still see. I felt a force pull me towards the fog. I gulped and slowly took a step. There were trees on either side of the path, and birds, lots of birds. What the hell is it with these birds? I kept walking, would this brick path ever end? Then I heard a roaring noise that sounded like water. I stepped through the light fog and stood in front of a massive waterfall feeding into a river. It must've been over 100 feet tall. The waterfall was being enjoyed by many birds. They were bathing and drinking. The sight was breathtaking, but also intimidating. Why were there so many birds around the castle? The Temulus controlled a multitude of animals, but couldn't they manage all these birds? As I kept thinking about my many questions, I walked towards the water.

No sooner I had reached the edge of the river than I felt a swirl and a gust of wind. It knocked me over. I turned around and there in front of me was the Brindle. Its enormous wings flapping to keep it in place, and talons that looked ready to crush me. It was massive. It stood about 20 feet tall, and its head was the size of my body. Its beak looked incredibly sharp, and as I slowly tried to back away it let out an ear-piercing squawk. It sounded like a cross between an eagle and a lion's roar. What was this thing? I covered my ears and head with my arms and curled into a ball. The force of the Brindle 's wings still keeping me down. After what seemed like minutes, it slowed its wings and landed a few feet from me. I could see the Brindle out of the corner of my eye. I was too afraid to uncurl myself from the pathetic ball I was in as I lay next to this magnificent creature.

I proceeded to sit up. The Brindle was perched on the ground looking at me. I didn't want to make any sudden movements. I stared at the Brindle and he let out another piercing squawk. Good grief! What did it want? I kept my eyes locked on it as I stood up. Obviously the Brindle didn't want to attack me or eat me, or it would have done so already. It cocked its head to the side as if trying to understand. I took a step closer and its wings fluttered slightly. I extended my arm and moved in even closer. It didn't take its eyes off me. It was beautiful and the most insane creature I had ever seen. I was drawn to it and I think it was drawn to me, too.

I was close enough to touch it. I reached out and felt its chest and beautiful feathers. My pink energy began to glow from my hands. What was happening? I quickly pulled my hand back and the charge subsided. I reached out again and the closer I got to the Brindle, the more my hands would glow. Holy hell! How was it doing this? I put my hand on its chest and the Brindle let out a roar and extended its wings as wide as it could. My electric charge pulsed out of my hand and surrounded it. I was in awe and my breathing was heavy. The Brindle retracted its wings and lowered its head close to me. I didn't know what to do. I was in shock, confused, it was as if this creature was able to amplify my power. We connected. I reached out to touch its head and, to my surprise, I was able to read its thoughts. It was a male. His name was Creed. He knew my name, and he knew who I was...this mystical creature knew who I was! Was there anyone or anything who didn't know me? How was I the last to figure this all out? I gulped and took in a deep breath.

"Penelope! Are you out here?" I heard a voice call out. Creed drew his wings ready for flight and took off. I looked up at the sky and back over my shoulder. Behind me was Mara.

"Mara, I...I am sorry. I needed some fresh air. All of this has taken me through a whirlwind of emotions." I sighed.

"His name is Creed."

"I know..." I replied.

"You know, we haven't seen him in a long time. He helped us a long time ago, but when we were defeated, he vanished. That was until Ford told us about you." Mara smiled.

"The day Ford saved you from The Port, we heard Creed's cries over our castle. It was a cry of hope, and we knew that you were someone that existed. I know Ford told you some of our story, and some of how you might fit into that, but there is more to it. Penelope, I'll take you to get something to eat, and we will help you understand.

Mara and I walked down a long hall and into a dining room. There was a long table with many chairs. The pictures on the walls depicted the Temulus and Neons at war. The succession of paintings showed blood, murder, and suffering. I walked along the wall looking at the paintings and the markings. Towards the end, there was a painting of Creed, a woman, and a Temulus warrior by their side. Such beautiful art, but truly unlike anything I had ever seen before, I was almost creepy. I sat down at the table with Mara. Three maidens brought us soup and charcuterie.

"Could I please have some more tea?" I requested. As I drank my tea, Mara began to tell me a story.

"I know this has been hard for you, and extremely confusing. We had hoped Ford would help ease some of your worry and anxiety. When he found you, he immediately told us and I knew we had to keep you out of harm's way. Most of that meant telling you the truth about who and what you are. Penelope, you have the power of a Neon. Your power just so happens to be rather powerful. It's not denoted by the green that the rest of us have. Yours is pink. While that's still a mystery for us, there is no doubt that you have Neon blood. That is why you are able to do what you do."

I nodded my head in understanding. Ford had told me this.

"Penelope, I also knew your father."

I put my tea down and my eyes widened.

"My father? My father, Guy Ash, the commercial realtor out of Charlotte, North Carolina? The one who has cared for me since I was a baby?"

Mara looked away and took a deep breath. She looked at me from the corner of her eyes and moved to my side of the table.

"Penelope, Guy Ash...He is a great man, and a great man that protected you and your mother. Especially, when your mother was sick."

My eyebrows furrowed. Why was Mara talking about my mother, and how did she know she was sick?

"Guy Ash was someone we entrusted to watch over the both of you after our war with the Temulus. You needed protection, your mother, Arynia, needed protection."

My eyes widened. I hadn't heard my mother's name in a long time. Let alone from someone saying it in the context of this world.

"What do you mean Guy Ash was entrusted?" I glared.

"Penelope...Guy isn't your father. He is someone from your world that we chose to be a guardian for us. Guardians are people that know who we are, believe in us, and are willing to sacrifice their life for us. Guy is, and has been, your guardian. He was your mother's, as well."

Mara's words were drowned out as a ringing in my ear began to take over. All the sounds in the castle melted away, and I could hear myself breathing in my head. I felt a sense of anxiety overcome me and my chest began to tighten. I was staring past Mara at the door. I needed to get out of here. I needed to get away from what she was telling me. How could my father not be my father? Was she crazy? I've known my father since I was a baby...or, I've known Guy. I couldn't breathe anymore, I was wheezing, and I stood up and ran towards the door.

"No. No. This isn't right." I whispered to myself as I stumbled to the door and ran out.

"Penelope, wait! Please!" Mara yelled.

How do I get out of here? The walls seemed to be closing in on me. My breathing was still erratic. I ran out of the door back into the garden. How the hell do I get back to campus? I needed to talk to Ronnie and Lyla. I needed to speak to someone who wasn't some mystical being. I needed my friends. I ran past the waterfall with tears streaming from my eyes.

Suddenly, Creed swooped in and landed in front of me. I dropped to my knees and lowered my head. He lowered his head next to mine and nudged my arm with his beak. My energy lifted out of me. I touched his head and he immediately knew what I was thinking, and I knew what was coursing through his mind. I stood up and tugged on his wing. He hoisted me on top of his back and took off into the sky.

Within seconds, I was transported back to campus. I was standing in front of the arts building, but Creed was nowhere to be seen. What had just happened? Did I do this, or did he? Where had he gone? Had anyone seen us? I shook off these questions and started walking towards the dorm. Tears dried on my face as I thought about what Mara had told me.

It was late, but I knew Ronnie and Lyla would be eating dinner. I stood outside the dorm for a few minutes and then called them on their phones. They ran outside to meet me.

"Penelope!" Lyla exclaimed.

"Pen!" Ronnie yelled. "Where the hell did you go? Where have you been? We've been calling you nonstop. I texted you a million times. What is going on? Vel said you were with Ford last night. Did he do something to you?"

"No! Ronnie, I'm fine. Just let it go. I've had a weird night and even weirder day. I just need to be around my friends."

Ronnie looked at me, confused, and shook his head in disappointment.

"Pen, of course! Come eat with us." Lyla gave me a hug. "We're going to dinner a block over at Clandestine. Apparently, the food is good and the menu always changes. We *have* to try it out!"

Great, could anything else around here be named anything more cryptic? I nodded and agreed. I wanted to tell them what I had just discovered, what was going on with Ford, what was going on within me, about Malee! But I couldn't. If I did, that would only put them in danger. We arrived at Clandestine, sat down for dinner, and I ate in silence.

PETAL

Chapter 9 – Blooming

After dinner, Ronnie offered to walk me back to my dorm room. I was quiet on our walk home. Lyla had headed up to bed and I stopped before the front door and sat down on the steps. Ronnie sat next to me and looked at me with worry on his face. He took my hand and looked at me with more concern than I had seen since our break up years ago. He was upset.

"Penelope, please tell me. Is everything okay with you? Ever since we got here, you've been acting strange, disappearing with Ford, and you just seem really upset. I'm your friend and you always tell me everything." It was dark all around us with some stragglers making their way back to the dorms. The stars were shining bright in the sky. I looked up to admire them as a tear streamed down my face. I was overwhelmed and I didn't want to talk about anything. I leaned in and put my head on his shoulder. He put his arms around me and held me as I cried. Ronnie knew not to ask me anything when I didn't feel like talking. All I needed was for him to hug me and be there for me. I had so much on my mind. Classes were starting in the next couple of days, and I needed to have my head on straight. As much as it could be at least. We sat there for about an hour before I stopped weeping and told Ronnie I was okay to go to my room and sleep. He was a little protective and insisted on walking me to my room. We got to my room and I gave him another hug and thanked him, and then we said good-night.

I turned around to open the door and I walked inside. The lights were on but Vel wasn't in her bed. Maybe she had a late dinner. I wondered if I should wait up since she would probably wake me up anyway when she got home. I sat in bed and reached back towards my bookshelf. The Divergence of Greek Rulers. Hm, that seemed a little fitting. I pulled it out and began to read.

It was about 10 pm, an hour after I had gotten back to our room, and Vel still wasn't back. I figured I could try and look for her and let her know I was okay. I had stormed away from her earlier that morning and I didn't want her to think any of it was her fault. I opened the door and walked down to the front of our dorms. It was dark out, and I wasn't exactly sure where I should begin to look for her. She said that she was part of a sorority, so maybe I could head over there and check. I wondered why she didn't live in the house. Maybe living with so many girls was annoying for her, just as it had been for me to meet her as my roommate. What was it with her loud music and obnoxious pink decorations? Okay, Pen, you're being rude. Just go look for her, and let her know you're not mad. I started in the direction of the sorority house we had gone to for the masquerade party.

Once I arrived, I could hear loud music coming from the backyard. Of course, she was probably partying and drinking. She had bragged about it to Lyla and Ronnie when they first met at breakfast. I decided to let myself in through the fence gate and look for her. I wasn't much in the mood to meet new people and stay for the party. When I walked into the backyard, the music was blaring, but nobody was there. Okay, so they decided to blast loud music and stay inside? Strange. I walked around the backyard, past the herb gardens and to the back door. I placed my hand on the doorknob and felt an eerie feeling wash over me. I hesitated to open the back door, but I had to find Vel. I gently opened the door and let myself in. Nobody was downstairs, but I could hear voices upstairs. I wasn't sure who it was, but I didn't want to scare anyone, so I called out.

"Vel! Is that you? It's Penelope. I came looking for you, figured you might be here!"

I didn't get a response, but the commotion from the bedroom faded away. It was quiet. Even the music had stopped. I stood in the living room looking up at the stairs.

"Velaire?" I called again, "Are you up there?" Still no response. I decided to walk up the stairs. Somebody was home and for whatever reason they weren't answering. I made my way to the stairs and put my foot on each wooden step. Each creaked loudly as I climbed to the second floor of the house. I got to the top and down to my left was a door that was partially open. I made my way to the front of the door and slowly pushed it open.

"Pen!" Vel was sitting in a chair having a glass of wine. Across from her was a guy I hadn't met. He looked much older. He stood up to shake my hand.

"Penelope, I'm Sam Harding," he said in a beautifully deep voice. He was of average height—maybe 5'10" or so. His eyes were a dark brown, his hair sandy blonde and well groomed. He wore a black sleeveless shirt and dark jeans. He wasn't muscular, but of average build. His overall size made me feel more comfortable for some reason. Finally, someone with a common name and familiar appearance.

"I'm Penelope," I managed to say.

Vel smiled. "Sam and I were just talking about the next event we are going to have."

I smiled. "Vel, I just came here to check on you, and to tell you that I'm sorry for running out on you this morning."

"Pen! It's okay! No big deal. Stay, sit with us and brainstorm." Vel moved over to the bed.

"Do you drink?" Sam asked me.

"Sometimes, I guess." I answered nervously. There was something about Sam. He wasn't extravagantly attractive, but he was polite, and nice...why was I feeling nervous around him? Not as nervous as I was around Ford, but it was different. Sam handed me a glass of wine. I decided I'd at least drink one glass.

"Where is everyone?" I asked.

"It's the last Saturday night before classes start! Everyone is at a party down the street at Sam's old frat house. We snuck away to take a break." Vel giggled.

As I sat there drinking my wine and conversing with Vel, Sam never took his eyes off me. He was studying me, in an uncomfortable, but intriguing way. I asked "So, Sam, how long have you been at Duke?"

"This is my last semester." He answered. "I'm finishing up my MBA in Leadership this year."

I smiled and looked back at Vel. Good grief, what was up with all these MBAs. She motioned towards him and mouthed something I couldn't make out. Great, was she trying to set me up with him? That's the last thing I needed. Or maybe I just needed less drama. Ford was drama. It followed him, or did it follow me?

"Penelope?" Sam broke my concentration. "Are you all right?"

"Yeah, I'm fine. Sorry." I drank my wine and set the glass on the side table. "I should go, it's been a long day and I'm kinda tired." I stood up and Sam stood up at the same time.

"Let me walk you out." He extended his arm and showed me the door.

"Uh, sure." I raised an eyebrow at Vel.

"Hurry back, Sam, we have to head back to the party!" She yelled out.

As we walked down the stairs Sam kept his eyes fixated on me. We got to the door and Sam stopped me. "Penelope," He said in his deep voice. "I know we just met, but maybe you and I can have lunch some time. Maybe tomorrow?" I gave him a half smile as I opened the front door. And there, on the other side, was Ford. He was standing on the front stoop. He looked annoyed. Sam looked at him in surprise.

"Penelope. Let's go." Ford demanded.

I was still upset from the whole Malee, Sarina debacle. My jealousy had gotten the best of me with him so worried about Malee, even though she had the power to protect herself. I used that to my advantage.

"Ford. This is Sam. He's a friend of Vel's, and ex-head of the frat house down the street."

Sam extended his hand. Ford had no choice but to shake it. I was smiling inside.

"Ford. Do you want to stay for a drink? Penelope, how about another?" I squinted my eyes knowing Ford would be extremely concerned by the fact that I had been drinking with someone else.

"No. Thanks. Penelope and I are leaving." Ford reached out for my hand and took it. He quickly pulled me out of the doorway.

"Bye, Sam. Nice meeting you. Thanks for the drink," I managed to say as we rushed down the steps and walked quickly through the school courtyard to my dorm. Ford kept his eyes forward, and made me keep up.

"Ford! Stop!" I yelled. "What are you doing? What is your problem?" I planted my feet firmly. "I'm not going anywhere with you."

"Penelope. Why were you at that house? Alone. Drinking with some random guy?"

"He's not some guy. I went looking for Velaire! She was there too. She was upstairs!" I argued. "You left me at your parent's house while you went to handle whatever you needed to handle with Sarina and Malee. What was I supposed to do? Stay stuck in some castle with people I don't know?"

"Penelope." He walked up to me and placed my chin in his hand. "I'm trying to keep you safe. I left you there because I knew my parents could protect you."

"Oh, yeah? And did you know that your parents knew my mother? Did you know that my dad isn't really my dad? Did you know that he was just some guardian sent by your people to protect me?" I started to tear up.

"Penelope, I had no idea. My parents hadn't talked to me much about your mom and dad. I came back to The Kingdom to check on you, and my mother said you had taken off. I was worried." He lifted my face and looked in my eyes.

I pulled his hand away. "I'm fine. I'm not staying with your parents. My friends are here, my life is here at Duke."

"I get it. I was trying to protect you the best way I knew how. Now that he..." Ford sighed. "Forget it"

"Now that he? He, who?" I asked.

"No one. I thought it was something, but it's not. Why were you drinking with this Sam guy?" Ford looked angry.

I looked at him, annoyed. "Sam is a nice guy who just wants to be a friend."

"Sam does NOT want to be your friend!" He raised his tone. "He wants more than that. It's obvious. I heard him invite you to lunch."

"Okay, so now you're just going to spy on me everywhere we go? You can't even tell Malee what is happening between us, but you sure as hell are quick to claim me when someone else tries to be nice to me!" I exclaimed.

"No! Well, not exactly," he replied.

"Maybe you and I just need to take a break from each other. Classes start on Monday and I really need to get my mind right." I took in a deep breath.

" Look. Okay, maybe I was a little jealous. I don't want another guy around you. I don't want them looking at you, or even thinking about you. It angers me that someone else wants what's mine."

"Yours? Who else knows that? Okay, so you've saved my life, you've helped me explore some of myself, my sexual self...and then what? At the first sign Malee or Sarina are in trouble you just drop me. Twice now! Ford. I need more than that. I *want* more than that!" I exclaimed.

"Penelope. I don't understand. You want more?" He was confused.

"Yes! Us together. You've shown me power I didn't know I had. Hell, a freaking charge lit came out of my mouth the last time we were together. I need to know what else I can do! I need to know how much more I can handle! Why won't you help me? I've shown you that you won't hurt me, and I want you, Ford. You said your dominance takes over. Show me."

Ford stood there as it started to rain. His hair was dripping wet. He took my hand and walked me towards his truck. We climbed in and drove to his house. He didn't say anything the whole ride there. Even when he opened the door and went to his bedroom to change, he was quiet. He offered me a clean shirt, his bed, and proceeded to sleep on the couch. I was really confused and also really tired. I figured he was still angry with me after meeting Sam. I decided to go to bed and talk with him in the morning.

I was mostly asleep, but heard a voice in my ear. I half opened my eyes to see Ford next to me. I could feel his lips breathing close to my cheek and my ear. I looked at the clock and it was 3:00 am. I thought I was dreaming. "Penelope." He whispered as I smiled. I could feel Ford between my legs. His bare hands caressing every inch of my back and down in between my legs where he grabbed on tight to my inner thighs. He pushed them open with his strong fingers. The same ones I had been longing to feel ever since he took my hand the first time. He began to kiss my knee and I felt his tongue slide up my right thigh. His moist tongue moved over my silk underwear and his lips slowly began to suck on my labia. He made circles with his mouth so as to massage my entire center. As he kissed me I could feel his fingers trickle towards my underwear and pull it out of the way. I was flowing with pleasure and could feel him use my wetness to lubricate my clit. I slowly opened my eyes.

"Ford..." I said in a moaning whisper as I grabbed his hair.

As soon as he heard me, he placed his mouth over my clit and began to suck with intensity. My body convulsed and I grabbed the sheets with all my might. I tipped my head back and moaned in ecstasy. His fingers were one thing, but his lips. So strong, so soft, so gentle. I wanted to enjoy this feeling. I was in a state of euphoria and my gasps of pleasure were proof. If anyone could make me feel like this it was him, only him.

I began to sit up but immediately felt my legs forced open. Ford had secured my legs to the bedposts. I could feel ropes close in on my ankles. The harder I tried to pull away the tighter the ropes became. Ford slid his hands from my thighs and caressed my hips. "Penelope. This is what you want? Me to take charge of you? You wanted more dominance." He gave me a gratifying smile and I gave him one in return. I was feeling a charge build up inside of me. He had unbuttoned my shirt while I was asleep. My breasts and hard nipples were completely exposed and I could feel a breeze blow over them. My inner sexual being was more than pleased. I wanted him to show me more. As he continued to hold my legs open, he positioned his tongue on my clit and made small circles with it. My body began to convulse. He was enjoying it. Taking his time. He let out a chuckle.

"Oh, no, not yet my Penelope. You wanted more. The other night wasn't enough for you. I'm not going to let you come just like this. As much as I want to, I'm also not going to go inside you until the time is right." All of a sudden, I heard a small drumming noise. I looked down and Ford had a small vibrator in his hand.

"Penelope. I want you to control your breathing and your desire. I want nothing more than to make you come right now, but I want your orgasm to be intensified."

Intensified? How much more could I feel? "I can't get enough of you." Ford whispered as he moved his nose close to my labia. He breathed in a deep breath. My wetness increased as he gently touched the tip of his tongue to me and tasted me. I tried to hold the feeling, but the urge to come was taking over my body. I could feel the power building and I wanted to release. Release myself all over him. I looked down at him and my heart and hands were glowing with a pink light. Ford looked at me and smiled.

He took the vibrator and began rubbing it around my neck. I closed my eyes, and my breathing picked up pace. My pink electric charge was emanating from my core. He slowly moved the vibrator over my breasts and around my erect nipples. They were so hard I felt I could probably cut glass with them. I groaned, attempting to pull my legs in, but the restraints wouldn't let me.

"Penelope. Your sweet moans. Say you're mine." Ford moved the vibrator further down to my inner-thigh. I whimpered. "Say you will be mine." His green energy pulsed through his veins he moved up to my lips and kissed me passionately. He took the vibrator and slid it over my labia. Gently tracing me he used my wetness to lubricate it.

"Ford! Yes, I will be yours." I yelled.

"That's right." He exhaled. He kept the vibrator on my clitoris and put his lips on mine to absorb my passionate cries. I felt a power rising inside of me. It was big and my core was filled.

"Penelope. Come for me," He whispered in my ear as he sucked on my ear lobe and tugged on it with his teeth.

My panting was sporadic. I hadn't felt this before. I hadn't explored this intense feeling let alone with sex toys. My hair raised on my arms. I was enjoying every second of this night. As he moved the vibrator faster over my clit I started to unravel beneath him. He hovered his hand over my mouth as I orgasmed and I let out cries of pleasure. This time, an electric charge exuded from my center. My stomach was radiating and light filled the room. It took a few seconds for the light to subside.

"You see that? That intensity. You only come for me, Penelope. Was that what you wanted?" He was out of breath as he licked his lips.

"Yes..." I moved my body around to shake off the orgasm. I watched Ford untie me with a smile on his face.

I felt powerful, but not in control. There was no way I could learn to harness this pillar of desire if I couldn't control my want for desire. "

"That bright light came out of me. What was it?" I asked him.

"Your sexual desire was manifested in your internal pulse of energy." Ford smiled.

"I liked that. A lot." I smiled and looked at him approvingly. He handed me his shirt. I slid it over my head and lay down in his bed. Ford lay in bed with me and began to ask me questions.

"So, my mother told me that you 'escaped' from the castle."

"I didn't escape! It would only be an escape if I had been a prisoner. And I wasn't a prisoner...right?" I toyed.

"Of course not." Ford nodded his head at me.

"I'm kidding. Yes, I left The Kingdom. I needed to be around my friends. Especially, after your mom had told me..."

"About your mother and Guy? Yeah. Penelope, I had no idea. I'm so sorry." Ford stroked my hair.

"Ford. It's okay. I guess it could've been worse. But...that means I don't know who my true father is. That scares me, but it also makes me really sad." I closed my eyes.

"Ok, well. How did you manage to get out of The Kingdom? Is there some transporting or teleporting power you have that I don't know about?" Ford teased.

"Well, interestingly enough. It was...Creed."

"Creed? But how? How did you...?"

"I don't know. The first time I saw him I felt drawn to him. So, when you took me back, I went looking for him. He didn't try to hurt me. He helped me transport back to my world. I don't know how, but when I touch him...my powers are amplified. My electric charge surrounds him, and he glows and he gets big, and I don't know what else." My eyebrows furrowed trying to make sense of it. Ford smiled and kissed me. "I told you Penelope. You're it. You're the one."

Chapter 10 - Darkness Awakens

The next morning, Ford drove me back to campus. I was still daydreaming about our night. The way he'd held me, the way he was so gentle but demanding all at the same time. Thinking about it made me want it all over again.

"Penelope, I'll tell Malee today. I will let her know there is no chance we will ever get back together. I will tell her that it's all you now. There is no more her and me." He spoke as he parked his armored truck in front of my dorm. I smiled and hugged him before getting out. "I'll pick you up later."

"Okay. I should be done with Vel before dinner." I had plans to go with Vel to the gym and then to lunch after she had texted me after I had left the sorority house last night. Ford's engine roared as he took off. I was still smiling and proceeded to walk up to my room. As soon as I opened the door, Vel jumped out of her chair and came to hug me. Was she always this peppy? Geez. Sitting at her desk was none other than Sam. Great. Just what I needed to deal with after a perfect night with Ford.

"Hi Penelope." He stood up.

"Hey...Sam." I walked over to my bed and sat down. "So, what are you guys working on? Are we still going to the gym, Vel?"

"Yeah! Let me get my stuff from the shower!" Before I could say anything else, Vel skipped out of the room and left me alone with Sam. I took a deep breath and slowly exhaled.

"How was the rest of your night, last night?" Sam smiled, but in an eerily creepy way. I just wished he would leave.

"It was fine." I was short.

Not taking any hints, he sat back down on Vel's chair and began staring at me. It was the most strange few minutes I had ever had. I tried to busy myself by organizing my books, reviewing my class schedule, anything to make it seem less awkward. But, I could feel him continue to stare in my direction.

"What are you majoring in?" He finally spoke.

"I'm here for med school." I replied.

"Impressive. What plans do you have as a speciality?"

"Something in Pathology, I think." I pursed my lips.

"Ambitious. I like it." He raised an eyebrow while he played with a pen on Vel's desk. He crossed one leg over the other, looking at me as if I had something else to tell him.

This small talk was really exhausting. Where was Ve-laire? Why was she taking so long? "I'm going to go check on Vel, and make sure everything is all right." I half smiled.

Sam stood up. "I'm sure she's okay. Vel's a big girl." He started to walk towards me. What the hell was he doing?

"Yeah, okay. I'm going to need you to stop where you are." Sam stopped in his tracks and put his hands in his pockets.

"Penelope. I'm not going to hurt you."

I looked over at my nightstand and as I was about to reach for my phone, he lunged at me and grabbed my arms. He pulled them both behind my back and pushed me face first against the wall. My electric charge started to show, but before I could react he took a syringe from his pocket and stabbed my neck. "You have something I want," he said to me as I collapsed on the floor. I was out of breath, I was weak, and my vision was blurry. What did he inject into me? As I looked up to yell for help, Sam was gone. Vel had come back from the showers.

"Oh my God! Penelope! What's wrong? Are you okay?" Vel lifted me up and put me on my bed.

"I'm fine. It's fine. I just had a bad migraine and got dizzy. I must've stumbled."

"Where's Sam?" She asked.

I didn't want to tell her what had just happened. If Sam meant what he said, she would be in danger if she knew.

"He had to go take care of something at his frat house. Some emergency."

"Ha, boys. Probably some of them trying to fight each other because they end up as drunken fools." She laughed.

"Okay, well, anything you need. Let me know. Why don't we skip the gym and I go get you something to eat? You'll feel better after eating."

"Sure." I agreed reluctantly. I couldn't sit around with what Sam had done. I sat on my bed with a confused look and lost in thought.

"It won't take long. Maybe I'll get something from Clandestine's. Just lay down and relax. I'll be right back." Vel took off.

I wasn't going to lie down, especially while Sam was out there wanting who knows what from me. Plus, I was worried about what he had injected into my neck. I texted Ford but didn't get a response. I waited impatiently for Vel to get back. She returned a few minutes later with a grilled cheese and soup from Clandestine's. I took one bite and could barely swallow I was so anxious.

"I need some air." I motioned to Vel.

"Okay, yeah sure. Do you want me to go with you?" Vel sounded worried.

"No, I'll be fine." I responded.

I figured I would head in Malee's direction. All things considered, I had to tell Ford what had happened.

I got in my car and headed a few blocks over. Ford's truck was out front. I got out and started towards the door. I reached for the handle and as I tried to turn it Malee's mom opened the door.

"Oh hi! Penny, is it?" She asked coyly.

"Um, it's Penelope." I responded.

"Yeah, if you're looking for Malee, she's in her room with Ford. I'm leaving to get my hair and nails done."

I entered the condo and walked towards the back . I could hear muffled voices in Malee's room. I was bracing myself for anything Malee had to say about Ford and me. I knew she wouldn't be pleased. As I came to the door, I could hear Malee.

"Ford. I know you miss me," she said in a pleading voice. "Don't you remember the fun we had. The time we almost…" Malee stopped when she heard me open the door.

As I looked in the room I could see that Ford was sitting on the bed, and Malee was trying to lean in and kiss him.

He stopped her and was about to speak but, by now, my blood was boiling. How could she try to pull something like that? He had come here to tell her it was over between them and she was just ignoring him. I threw the door open and, in a blind rage, lunged at Malee. My strength was unmatched. I felt an intense energy and I grabbed Malee by her neck and pinned her against the wall. I stared in to her eyes.

"Pen...aaghaa" She gasped.

"Penelope! Don't!" Ford demanded. "Let her go!"

Wait, was he protecting her? If so, he could forget it. My grip tightened around her neck and my power increased. I could see my reflection in her eyes, and I was smiling. My eyes began to darken and a red fire was burning inside of them. Malee had fainted.

"Penelope!" Ford struck me with a green pulse and I was thrown to the ground.

"Malee! Malee! Can you hear me?" Ford shook her then gave her CPR. He tried for several minutes until she finally awoke gasping for air.

I sat on the floor confused and in some pain. My mind was racing and my breathing was erratic. I looked up at Ford and then Malee. "I...I'm sorry. I don't know what happened. I've never done anything like this before. I didn't..." I stopped myself and quickly got up to run out of the room.

"Penelope, wait!" Ford yelled after me.

I was scared. Somehow, a rage inside of me had taken over and I had almost killed Malee. I didn't understand. I stood outside in the crisp air looking around, gripping my hair, tears falling down my cheeks. Ford came running out.

"Penelope."

I didn't respond.

"Penelope!" He put his hands on my shoulders.

"Don't touch me!" I kept on crying.

"Penelope. It's okay. It's okay. I'm here." Ford hugged me.

"What did I just do?" I yelled hysterically.

"She'll be okay. She'll be okay." I kept whispering to myself, and Ford walked me to his truck. We got inside and he held my hand. In that moment, he transported us back to

The Kingdom. He walked me down the long corridor to a large bedroom and sat me down on the bed.

"Here." He handed me a blanket. "This would be your room if you had stayed. It still is, if you want it."

I was lost in thought. Frozen. Staring at the ground.

"I'm going to get you some tea." Ford left and came back with Winsten and Mara some minutes later.

"Penelope. Are you okay?" Mara asked me. I looked up at her.

"I...I almost killed her." I spoke in a soft tone.

"Ford told us what happened." Mara offered me some tea.

"Penelope. Ford told us he could see red reflected in Malee's eyes. We need you to tell us how that happened." Winsten sat down on a chair in front of me. Ford walked over and set next to me on the bed. I took a sip of tea and looked at Mara. She nodded her head.

"I wanted to go to Malee's to see Ford, and to make sure Malee didn't hate me for what Ford had just told her."

Winsten looked at Ford questioningly.

"Father, I had gone over there to let her know that I was going to be with Penelope, and that out relationship was over." Ford sighed.

"Go on, Penelope." Winsten looked at me.

"I heard them talking, I saw Malee try to kiss him, and rage took over. I became angry. It was like a darkness washed over me and took control of my emotions. I knew I was gripping her neck, but I didn't want to let go. It was almost as if I had become someone else ."

Winsten sighed heavily. "What about the red?"

"The red light. It came from my eyes. I felt it consume me when I looked at Malee. Ford, I'm sorry, I'm so sorry." I started to cry again.

"Penelope. It's okay. Malee is okay. I called her mother a few minutes ago to have her take Malee to the hospital. I told her she had slipped and fell down the stairs when she came outside to say goodbye to me. She will be okay." Ford hugged me.

" I know you're still in shock, and that this is hard for you, but can you think of the last time you felt this way?" Mara asked me.

"Never! Never." I immediately answered. "Not until..." I hesitated and took a deep breath.

"Until what, Malee?" Ford urged me.

"Sam."

"What about Sam?" Ford became angry.

"Who is Sam?" Winsten asked.

"When Ford dropped me off earlier today, my roommate Vel was there along with a guy I met yesterday. He's friends with Vel, and supposedly heads one of the frat houses on campus. Vel and I were supposed to go to the gym today, and she went to get her things. While she was out of our room he told me he wanted something from me, and then forcibly injected something into my neck with a small syringe."

Ford was breathing loudly. He was livid. "I'm going to kill him." He attempted to leave.

"Ford, wait." His mother called out. "We need to fully understand who this Sam person is, and find out what he injected into Penelope."

Ford was pacing back and forth. His hands in fists.

"Penelope, do you have any idea where Sam could be?" Mara asked.

"No, but I know who might." I answered.

"NO. No way you're going to find him, or talk to Vel. I won't let you." Ford interjected.

"Ford, we *have* to find Sam. He will have our answer. He won't be easy to bring in, given he already knows Penelope will try and find him," Winsten confirmed.

"Fine, but I'm staying with you." Ford demanded.

"Ford, no. I'm fine. I'll go back to my dorm since Vel is probably looking for me, and I want to try to get some information out of her. She will know where Sam might hang out, or where I can find him." I stood up. "Take me back."

"Penelope, take care of yourself. As soon as you find where he might be, let Ford know, immediately." Mara demanded.

Instantly, Ford and I were back at Malee's apartment. I took my car and drove back to campus. Ford followed closely behind. As I walked towards my dorm, Ford parked his truck and kept his eyes on me. I looked back and gave him a nod. When I walked back into my room, Vel was sitting next to her empty food tray from Clandestine's.

"Well, I finished my food. The grilled cheese is on your desk. I thought you didn't feel well enough to get up, but I guess not. You were gone for long enough." She was annoyed.

"Vel, I'm sorry. I started feeling a little better after I got some air, and I just wanted to say hi to my friends. I saw Ronnie outside and we ended up talking longer than expected. I felt bad, especially since we missed the gym this morning. Here take my 20 bucks. At the very least I can pay you back."

"Fine. No biggie. I forgive you." She smiled at me.

"Vel, can I ask you something?"

"Yeah, sure, shoot."

"Do you know where I could maybe find Sam?" I asked shyly.

"Ha! Sam? So you're into him! OMG, this is exciting. Yes!" Vel was jumping up and down.

173

"No, not really. Well, I just want to maybe take him up on his offer for lunch."

"He asked you to lunch!" She exclaimed. "Well, not sure where he might be right now. He could be at his frat house." I wondered if he would be there after what he had done. "Or, actually, sometimes he likes to head down to the library and read some Mark Twain. At least that's what he tells me."

"Vel, thank you. I'm going to stick this food in the fridge...and, I'll be back later!" I swept out of the room.

Ford was still sitting in his truck waiting for me. I ran over to his passenger side window.

"Vel says he frequently goes to the library. So, I'm guessing he'll either be there, or at the frat house. I think the library is definitely worth a shot."

"Let's head over there," he said as he got out of his car.

We walked briskly past all the student buildings and lines of students signing up for activities. If only every-thing could have started out normal for me, too. I could've been one of those students signing up. I looked back hesi-tantly, but then remembered I must have a bigger purpose heading to where I was with Ford. When we got to the library there was caution tape around it.

"What? What happened?" I asked a security guard who was rolling out more tape.

"A small area of the library has collapsed. No one was hurt, but it needs some rebuilding. Looks like there was a minor fire, but this library is so old it caused some wooden pillars to collapse. Hopefully it should be up in no time. The damage is minor, but still dangerous."

I looked over at Ford. "Now what? We have to get in there. Vel said Sam spends most of his time here. But why would he? Maybe we can find something that connects him to all of this."

"I know." Ford motioned towards the back of the building. We rushed across the grass and headed towards the back of the library.

Ford put his hands together and focused on igniting his energy. He slowly reached towards the cement wall and burned a hole through into the library. Holy cow! Is this what he can do with his power? Can I do that too? God, he looked so attractive. Okay, Penelope. Focus. He motioned for me to go inside. We ended up on the first floor inside a janitor's closet.

"Um, you couldn't make that hole, like, a little more to the left?" I joked.

"Yeah, libraries aren't my thing. Didn't have a map." He said with sarcasm.

We opened the door into a hallway. The emergency lights were on. The damage must have hit one of the power lines.

"Stay behind me." Ford walked in front of me towards the middle of the library. It was massive, and we were not even sure Sam was going to be in here. We continued walking towards the front, but not a soul was in sight. We walked down each aisle, but all was deathly quiet.

"Maybe he's not here. I mean, it *is* closed," I suggested. "They probably sent everyone home once the building collapsed."

"I don't trust that he wouldn't come in here anyway." Ford answered.

As we walked towards the stairs we heard some rustling coming from the second floor. We stood against the wall of the stairs and waited. After a few seconds we slowly made our way up the stairs. We walked by each aisle of books, stealthily looking for where that noise could've come from. We got to a back corner of the library where the shelves lined the back of a room. In the room there were couches, a TV, and a door in the corner. As we looked in the room from the bookshelves we saw Sam walking towards the door.

"He is here!" I whispered.

"I'm going to get him." Ford insisted.

"No! Let's watch and see what he does. Why would he be here when the library is closed? I mean, part of it collapsed. How is he in here?" I was curious and my suspicions were aroused.

We watched him for several minutes. Sam walked to the door. It was locked, but he pulled a key out of his pocket and unlocked it. How did he have a key to some door in the library? And what was he doing in a library anyway? He was supposed to be the frat guy that hosted insane parties with his friends, not some library rat. Surely that had to be a cover for whatever he was up to. Just then, his phone rang.

"Shh, shh." I looked at Ford who had moved closer to get a better look.

"Sir, yes. I was able to inject her with the suppressant. Project Nanolegion is underway."

I looked at Ford with my eyes wide.

"No sir, I haven't seen her yet. How do I know it worked? Because I know!" He yelled into the phone. "Stop questioning everything I do!" He hung up the phone.

Project Nanolegion? A suppressant? Suppress what? Sam slid a card through a scanner behind the door and an elevator door opened.

I motioned to Ford. "We have to follow him!"

"We can't! We don't know what's down there! We need to be smart." Ford directed.

Smart? I needed to get this Nanolegion, or whatever hell it was, out of me.

"Together we have insane powers and I don't understand why you don't want to follow him down there." I whispered loudly.

"Obviously he knows something not everyone else knows. He must know about your powers. He managed to inject you with some 'suppressant' which obviously means you're not able to defend yourself since you couldn't fend him off. No. We don't need to follow him down there right now. We need to be patient."

By the time Ford had finished his explanation, Sam was gone. Then Ford grabbed my hand and transported us back to The Kingdom.

"Ford! Seriously? You take us back here and you're okay with not knowing what suppressant is in me! Even if you are not worried, I am." I quickly ran behind him as he rushed to find Mara and Winsten.

"What is happening here? Is there news?" Winsten met us at an open door. I walked into their room. Mara sitting at a table with tea. "Come" She motioned. Each time I was here, I was in awe of their castle. I sat with Mara, and Ford stood talking quietly with his father.

"It's some sort of suppressant." I heard him say, "but I don't know for what. We saw Sam in the library. He was on the phone and there is some sort of secret chamber in that building." As Ford spilled the information to his father, both Mara and Winsten looked at each other. They did not speak.

Seeing the look between the two of them, Ford demanded of his father, "What? Do you know what it is? Do you know what substance is in Penelope?"

"Ford, Penelope. Remain calm," Winsten replied. "I think we *may* know what it is. Years ago, when we fought the Temulus, their ruby magic was their driving power but, as well, their warriors were armed with advanced technology. We don't know where it came from and we weren't sure of its purpose, at the time." Mara looked out the window.

Winston continued. "That is until our Neon warriors weren't able to draw their energy after coming in contact with this particular substance. Our warriors were stabbed or injected with some form of nanotechnology which neutralized their powers and made them almost non-existent. That was part of the reason the Temulus were able to control everything, and that is why we lost our control. This substance was unlike anything we had ever seen before, and we were powerless against it. It was a massacre."

My eyes widened in horror, it was hard to grasp the enormity of what Winsten was telling us.

"Except." Winsten added.

"Except what?" Ford was furious.

"Penelope, as I understand it, your powers are still with you, and you can use them at will." Mara asked. "Am I correct?"

Unable to speak, I merely nodded in agreement.

"Somehow, they've left it alone, either that, or they do not know the extent of your powers. From what I know, and making an educated guess, it seems more likely that they tried to *make way* for something to come to the surface by injecting her with a suppressant of Neon power."

I looked at Ford confused.

"What would they want, and why would they get this idea in the first place?" Ford was impatient.

"Ford. Both you and Penelope witnessed the incident with Malee. Penelope, you say you saw red in your eyes, and around your hands, well, you know that only means one thing…"

"Ruby?" I guessed, knowing how serious this now was.

Chapter 11 - Dual Danger

After speaking with Mara and Winsten, Ford transported us back to his apartment. Once there, he couldn't stop pacing around his kitchen. He seemed angry.

"Ford, you are making me more nervous than I already was. Good grief, sit down. What is up with you?" I spoke forcefully.

"Penelope. There's no way you have that evil inside of you. You can't. You belong to me. You're supposed to belong to me..." Ford anxiously responded. I couldn't understand what he felt.

"Ford, you're not making any sense." I shook my head.

"Listen to me, there's only one other person in these worlds, apart from you, who knows the depths of Ruby magic. I refuse to think that you are anything like him."

"*Like* him?" I asked.

"I didn't want to tell you about him when you asked me about it—I was being protective, and I didn't want you to know more than you could handle. My father thinks there's a possibility because of this whole thing with Sam..." Ford walked over to grab some glasses and a bottle of wine. He walked me over to his couch and turned on his fireplace.

I looked at him, almost feeling disappointed. I decided to ask him one more time. "Tell me. Tell me about it all. You promised...". He poured us some wine and then took a big gulp of his own. He took my face in his hands and stared into my eyes with a powerful fierceness.

"I will tell you. Now." He handed me a glass of wine.

"When the Temulus invaded, their leader, Horatio had a son whom he promised he would use to end our world. And not only the Neon world, but yours, too." I looked at Ford in shock and disbelief.

"This cannot be real! Tell me it isn't so!" I exclaimed.

"Oh, it's real alright, Penelope. His son...his name is Chez. Chez was born with a rare condition and was given only days to live when he was first born. He was on the brink of death, so Horatio took him to a place called The Depths of Shadows. They told him Chez would only live for one more day unless he used their Ruby magic to cure him. Horatio, as desperate as any parent would be, handed his son over to the Shadows and he never saw him again. Part of the agreement was that Chez would grow up under the care of someone else. Until a short time ago, Horatio only knew his son would live, but he did not know him, or who raised him. One day, Chez, a young man by then came knocking on the door of the Temulus and presented himself as Horatio's son. He was nicely dressed, clean-shaven, and looked as if he had lived a life of luxury. He was holding a talisman when he arrived. Horatio and Chez spent the next years renewing their relationship as father and son. It wasn't until Horatio defeated Danita with his talisman that we discovered that Chez had actually created the talisman to harness Ruby power." Ford paused for a moment and looked at me intently."

This story was becoming more and more complicated, and I was losing patience and understanding. Neons, fairy-tale castles, secret powers—it was all too much. "Tell. Me. Explain how that affects what you *think* is inside of me. I need to understand what all this means." I spoke in a tone that brooked no argument.

"If my father is right, Sam injected you with a serum that suppresses Neon energy in order to try and draw out the Ruby magic inside of you. Most likely, he used the same exact nanotechnology used in our war." Ford sighed. "Which means, obviously, he knows what you are, and believes that somewhere in you, you harbor the magical Ruby power. This power is as ancient thousands of years old. When you sign a deal with The Depth of Shadows, you sign your life away. Ruby magic can obliterate anything you want it to with just a mere thought. But it takes a certain person to be able to control it, so it doesn't control you, and you *turn*."

Frustrated, I began to lose my senses, my head hurt, and I was only focused on Sam and that damned secret elevator. "Clearly I'm not getting anywhere just sitting here." I retorted. I stood up to leave.

"Penelope, wait. Where are you going?"

"Listen, Ford, I know you want to protect me. Keeping me locked up in places is *not* going to help with that. I'm leaving, and you are going to let me, because I don't want you near me. I have learned a lot of new things within the last 48 hours that I don't care to think about right now other than to find answers to questions that barely make sense!" I grew increasingly impatient. "Take. Me. Home. Now."

Ford drove me from his hidden house in the woods to campus. It was late and the moon lit up the sky with immense power. I looked up and felt a few drops of rain hit my face as I got out of the car.

"Thanks Ford. I have to go."

He looked at me, sadness in his eyes.

I started in the direction of my dorm. I knew he'd be watching me intently until I was at my door and safely inside. I heard his car leave, waited a minute, and turned right back around to leave my dorm.

There was no way in hell I was going to sit back and wait for something to happen. I had only been at college for two weeks, and I had already met some crazy guy with powers, been targeted by ugly looking creatures, was injected with some random serum, and almost choked a girl to death! I marched towards the library. I didn't know what the hell I was going to do, but I knew I was going to do something. It was dark. I stood in front of the tall building and could still see the caution tape surrounding it. My heart was pounding and my palms were sweaty, but I was determined to press on. I walked around to the side where Ford had knocked out a hole. Ugh, it was the cleaning supply room, of course. I tripped over a bucket and winced. Surely I was making enough noise to cause someone to hear my presence! I kept walking and took the stairs to the room where we had seen Sam take an elevator. The library was quiet. There was no one around at this time of night, and the only light I had in front of me was that of my phone. I walked quietly up the stairs to the second floor.

All of a sudden, I realized I wasn't scared anymore. I didn't care who or what I would run into. All I cared about was getting answers. When I got to the room with the elevator, I could see that the door was slightly ajar. Had Sam been here again? Or maybe he had left it open? This was strange, but I wasn't going to miss an opportunity to find out what was down there. I stepped inside the elevator and looked around. There were only two buttons. One that read "Floor 1" and the other that read "Base Level." Well, I guess I was on Floor 1 given I had seen Sam go down in this elevator so I pressed the "Base Level" button. The elevator doors jerked closed and I started to slowly descend. It was taking longer than I expected an elevator to take if it was only going down one floor. After about 15 seconds the elevator came to a halt. The doors slowly opened and I could see a long hallway with bright lights. There were two big doors at the end of the hallway. I looked around and slowly stepped out. My senses were mixed with rage and frustration. Rage because of what Sam had done to me, and frustration because I couldn't quite protect myself yet. An eerie feeling fell around me as I left the elevator.

I took a deep breath, exhaled, and began walking down the long hall. I got to the doors and noticed a small fingerprint pad on the bottom right of the wall. Great. Now how the hell was I going to get in? I tapped the screen and an image came up "finger here". What the heck, I guess I could try and put mine. I had nothing to lose. I put my index finger against the fingerprint pad and the scanner moved across it.

"Accepted" read the screen. What? There was no damn way. As I stood there in shock, the two doors slid open and

I was met with another long hall with endless windows.
What in the world was going on? How did my fingerprint
open these doors and why? I looked at the corridor and
there were windows on both sides from top to bottom.
Well, here goes nothing! I stepped into the hall. I turned to
look out one of the windows and I was immensely
shocked. There was a vast jungle on all sides of me. Was
this a joke? Was this some other portal or dimension?
Please, I'd had enough of these worlds. But I guess I
couldn't expect this to be normal. I was below a college
library and had just walked into a hallway in the middle of
a jungle. Okay, Pen, what did you think you were going to
find? In that instance, as I walked towards the white door at
the end of the hallway, I heard the loudest squawk I had
ever heard. It sounded familiar. It couldn't be...

As I turned away from the white door and looked over
my shoulder to the window, I could see something familiar.
A Brindle was perched on a branch several meters away. It
was enormous. It was beautiful. But it wasn't Creed. This
Brindle had a dark red hue and scars on its face. It looked
tired. I walked up to the glass and pressed my hand against
it. Suddenly, the Brindle let out a loud howl and locked

eyes with me. I could feel her. She was trying to speak to me.

No sooner had I locked eyes with her than the white door opened. I turned back confused and startled. It was as if someone had opened it for me. I looked around and nodded at the Brindle. I walked through the door and entered an enormous lab. There was a central room with tools, machines, chairs, and medical equipment everywhere. I held my breath as I walked in the shadows of the top level. I was surprised to see such a big place hidden away below this library. I walked towards the stairs and saw, down three flights of stairs, someone talking with a doctor. It was none other than Sam. I immediately ducked and hid behind a desk. He was here, the person who had stuck me with a needle! Now that I had located him, there was no way in hell I was leaving here without some answers.

I saw them both start down a hallway below the stairs. I immediately stood up and started quickly down the stairs towards the same hallway. As I approached, I couldn't see them. I walked into the hallway and, just as quickly as entered, I was thrown across the hall against the wall by Sam. I stood up panicked and tried to make a run for it. Sam grabbed my hair and pushed me up against the wall pressing my hands behind my back. I could see the doctor out of the corner of my eye.

"Do it." Sam ordered him. "Now, Kyle."

The doctor, named Kyle by all appearances, took a needle out of his pocket and stuck me in the neck. I immediately fell over. I was awake! I could see everything! Except, I couldn't move.

"Pen, it's okay. Keep calm. It's just a paralytic dose of Brindle blood. You will be okay. You didn't think we were going to let you through here, did you? We have a very robust security system. You must've known."

A tear strolled down my face from anger.

"Or maybe you did know...Oh, Pen, don't cry."

Part of me knew it was dangerous to follow Sam, and I knew I would get into trouble. But part of me didn't care, and wanted to pursue answers no matter what, no matter the consequences. Sam carried me down the hall and opened a security door. My mind began to race. My heart was pumping with severe anxiety as I was carried to an operating table, and there I saw the most vile, unforgettable, grotesque visions imaginable. Was this the paralysis? Was I really seeing this? All around the room were capsules containing people...they were suspended in some sort of pink substance. The same pink of my aura. They were pale, their skin was thin, their eyes were closed, and I could see tubes draining blood from their bodies. I felt my heart sink deep into my body. This was not how I imagined I would die. There was nothing I could do. I couldn't move.

Sam laid me on the operating table and strapped my wrists and ankles to it. Another tear rolled down my face. He slipped a gag over my mouth.

"Penelope Ash," the doctor addressed me. "It is so nice to finally meet you, and in this manner! Who could ask for a better first impression. My name is Dr. Kyle. I own this lab, and Mr. Sam over here has been helping me keep track of you. I love that he was finally able to convince you to come down." Kyle walked around the operating table examining my hair, my feet, and my arms. He was tall and skinny with wavy dark brown hair. He wore a mask over his nose and mouth, and he was wearing tight blue scrubs. "You seem not to understand why you're even here which I'm guessing is why you came searching for answers. Alas!

I have disappointing words for you since it doesn't look like you'll be going anywhere anytime soon." He smiled as he looked at me. I was sick with anxiety thinking about what he was going to do to me. I needed to do something— but I couldn't move. Sam stood and watched from near one of the capsules, a smile on his face.

"So, as we have come to find out, you, my dear, hold a power that many want." He chuckled. "You see, my partner Sam here, injected you with our very own Nanolegion. It's a high dose suppressant that eliminates all this Neon magic crap you have in your system and allows other powers to flow through. We got word that you have some Ruby magic in you." He walked closer to me and smiled as he brushed the back of his hand against my forehead. He took a few strands of hair and sniffed them. "All those bodies over there. We were told they had Ruby magic just like you, so we tried to extract and drain their blood and plasma. It didn't work. Whoever gave us that intel was misinformed, and now sits 6 feet under, but at least we were able to use these Neons to discover the perfect suppressant for its power. It was a win, win! I'm sure they've been looking for them for years. Oh well, who knew! We know you're the real deal."

His voice trailed off and I began to feel a fire inside of me. If I could harness any pillars to help me right now they would have to be *energy* and *mind*. Previously, I had thought about my father to harness the *mind* pillar, and after finding out he was only a guardian I didn't have it in me to summon it. My mind went quickly to Ronnie and Lyla. My friends. Oh how I wish I could see them one last time. I didn't want to leave this world without saying goodbye, without spending time with them like I said I would, without one last hug.

As these thoughts filled my mind with memories, I could feel a tingle in my hands. I felt energy flow through my mind and down my arms as Dr. Kyle continued his psycho rant.

"We just need to extract the Ruby power you've got so we can make more of you! Pen, we don't want to kill you! We just want to find out what makes you, well, you. That way we can find out if you're replicable!" In that moment a full surge of pink filled my arms and I pulled away from the restraints. My hands were glowing. As I stared at them in shock, I quickly used the electric charge to send Kyle flying through the air. Sam grabbed me from behind and threw me across the room over the operating table. I landed against the mirror and felt a sharp pain in my side. I howled as the mirror broke into thousands of pieces and stabbed me in the back. My pink energy had become dull, but it was still present. Sam grabbed a piece of the mirror and ran towards me.

"Don't kill her!" Dr. Kyle yelled from behind him. As Sam fell against me, the sharp mirror in his hands dug into my arm. The pink aura that remained inside me shocked him and sent him into a full-blown seizure. Both Sam and Kyle were on the floor, which is where I wanted them, but I couldn't handle the pain. I couldn't get up. I looked over the lab and saw syringes of paralytic. I slowly stood up, blood running down my body. Applying pressure on my wound, I stumbled and grabbed one syringe and quickly stuck it in Sam's neck. I turned around to get the other for Dr. Kyle, but he was suddenly nowhere to be seen. I had to decide whether to stay and try to find and inject the doctor, or get the hell out of here. My white shirt was completely blood stained, and I knew I was losing a lot of blood. I began to feel weak and dizzy. I made a snap decision and headed back towards the lab and up the stairs, through the hallway, up the elevator, and out of the library. It was dark. I couldn't yell, my energy was draining, and I figured if I could make it to the side of the road...

I was exhausted, running across campus in the dead of night. I had to make it to the road where I could see lights and cars driving by. I kept looking behind me with painful tunnel vision. I stumbled and watched my blood drip down my hands as I held my back. My sight became dull and my breathing labored. I couldn't run anymore, my legs were giving in struck with the feeling of painful needles all down my calves. I fell to my knees and put my head down to cry. Those bodies, what human could do such a thing to innocent lives? They weren't human was my answer. All those Neons, their blood was just draining, their faces were imprinted in my mind. I laid on the cold wet pavement, my shirt torn, my pants ripped to shreds, and rain camouflaging my tears. Hitting me like a million tiny icicles the sting consumed every inch of my body. I could see cars driving by, high beams on, slowly climbing the roundabout that hid my body. This is where I thought it would end. This is where I thought he would find me, finish me, kill me.

My energy, my glow, was dimming with every small rock being washed away by the rain. The pain was unbearable. My arms and legs were bruised from the fight, and my nose bleed was a mere pink tint from the rain on my face. My clothes stained red.

One...two...three...four...How many cars would pass by without noticing my white shirt glistening in their headlights? I couldn't speak, my eyes seemed to stare into the darkness forgetting to blink, I couldn't even think in my own words. My words felt borrowed when I tried to free them from my lips. Even if I called out, would they hear me? Would someone help me? How long had it been? I closed my eyes. My mother...oh how I missed her voice, her smell, her hair, her soft embrace when she comforted me. I drifted off.

What seemed like minutes passed and I slowly opened my eyes. I felt two arms reach under me and lift me with gentleness and power. Trying to make out who it was that had saved me, all I could sense was his rage and, in that moment, I knew.

"Pen, relax for me, baby. You will be okay," he said...and, in one second, we were gone.

Chapter 12 – Chez

I slowly opened my eyes. The thread of light stung my face every time I blinked. I looked around and began to panic. I was in a large bedroom with curtains that hung to the floor, and then I noticed that the color red adorned every corner, including the velvet pillows on the bed and the silk sheets. I didn't understand. I immediately thought about last night and felt my side and my back. I yanked the covers off. What! Nothing...no scar, no pain, no bandage, nothing. I was confused and my head hurt. I looked for my clothes, but instead found a red dress lying on a chair. I quickly grabbed it and headed for the door. I was in a huge house. One that I didn't know. I ran down the hall and came to a door, which lead to a main corridor. From there, I could see two enormous doors that would surely lead me outside. Before I could take a step forward, I froze.

Where was I? What was I going to do? I remembered last night in amazing clarity, but who had saved me? Ford? I slowly backtracked towards the bedroom and saw a door ajar to what looked like an office. I opened the door and walked inside. Around the office were several war plaques and medals. In fact, they were everywhere. One that read *For the War on the 3rd* and another *Leader of the High Power.* In the middle of all of them was a picture of a tall, muscular, dark haired man. He looked commanding, he looked intimidating. I walked up to the picture and read it. "*Chez Dreneau - 1st warrior.*" I instantly began to panic. I rushed out of the office and ran downstairs towards the doors. No sooner had I placed my hand on the doorknob than something in me made me stop. Again, I felt myself wanting to head back toward the bedroom. It was a feeling, a connection. I slowly walked back upstairs and re-entered the room. Chez was standing in front of the bed with his back to me. I didn't want to run away. There was something drawing me to him. How the hell had I ended up here? Had he kidnapped me? I slowly walked over to him and, as I was about to place my hand on his shoulder, he quickly turned around and pinned my throat against the wall with his hand and stared into me with his fierce red-lit eyes. I was stunned. Letting out a deathly howl he slid one of his hands along the buttons of my shirt. His lips closed around the underside of my chin.

For a split second I wanted him...but then the feeling passed. What was wrong with me?

"Chez, please don't." I spoke faintly, and I began to regret my decision of running out that door. Was he going to kill me?

He held my head against the wall with his hand on my throat.

"I finally have you— in the flesh." He sniffed my neck. "I thought this is what you wanted. You wanted me to help you. To have you. To own you."

I didn't understand. He hugged me and sniffed my hair, inhaling and exhaling. Breathing me in.

"That's why I saved you and kept you. I made the decision for you. Except, you aren't a prisoner. You could have escaped, but you stayed. You surprise me."

"What do you mean you saved me?"

"Yes, I saved you. You've been more or less uncon-scious for two days, sleeping." He growled. He grabbed me and forcefully shoved me onto the bed.

"What? No, it was Ford? He saved me. Where is he? What did you do to him?" I yelled.

"I wasn't the one that left you on the side of the road, almost dead! I wouldn't do that to you, my sweet Pen." He walked closer to me.

"But, Ford. I saw his eyes, I felt him, I heard him talk to me!" I started to panic.

"Pen. All of that was simply your power deciding what to think, what to feel and hear. This is the power you have when you're with Ford, but that's not *all* you are. You can be so much more. You *have* so much more, and I can help you release it."

I furrowed my eyebrows. "What happened to all my cuts? My bruises! All the blood!" I kept raising my voice.

"Pen, you healed yourself. Well, with a little help from me." He smirked. "Ruby magic is very tricky. When it starts to take over, it starts to make you go crazy. You don't know real from fantasy. Unless you learn to control it! It's an immense power." He chuckled.

I started for the door in shock. How had he *helped* me?

"No!" His speed was unmatched. Red was coursing through his veins. He held the door shut and proceeded to lock it. He held my arm tightly and forced my back against the wall. "You're not leaving. You need to know, sweet Pen, that I can give you everything you want. Everything you need. Mind, body, and soul." He whispered with his lips close to my ear.

Why hadn't I left when I had the chance? Why hadn't I escaped when I could? Who *was* this guy? Part of me was curious. Part of me could feel the red inside of me. A red that was drawn to Chez. Almost as if this red made me another person altogether. This other person looked at his towering figure with nothing but darkness protruding through his eyes. But there was something about him. Something inside of me found him alluring. He was nothing like Ford, and all I could remember was how the Temulus had destroyed half the Neon world with a talisman Chez had created!

"Pen, we would be so perfect." He stroked my cheek. "Just you...and me."

I pulled my cheek away and looked down at the ground. I could feel my hands burning pink, but there was no way my power was a match for him. Ruby magic would obliterate me. Even if I had that stuff in me, I didn't know how to control it. And going up against the leader *of* it, there was no way I would be victorious.

"So then, you should've escaped when you had the chance, Penelope." He smiled at me with a maniacal grin.

"Would you like to know what you would be escaping? Here, let me show you." He put his hand out for me to take it. "Take it." He demanded.

I held out my hand as Chez walked me to his bed and sat me down. He ordered me to close my eyes and enter his mind.

"What better way to show you than to project some ideas into your head." He responded excitedly.

We were in a bungalow on a deserted island. The waters were clear, the sky was blue, and Chez was gazing at me. His strong demeanor and his chiseled abs were glistening with water. His subtle goatee dripping from the shower he had just taken. He wore only pants. He took a towel and began to dry off the excess water from his body and face.

"Penelope. It's okay. Come."

He took my hand and hoisted me on the breakfast table. I complied. At that moment, I wanted Chez. He was endearing and mysterious. His eyes were glowing a slight red and his hands raised to meet my face. He drew closer and began to furiously kiss me.

He whispered in my ear. "Penelope. I'm going to have you. Whatever it takes for you to be mine."

Just then, the other side of me began to take over and my eyes began to glow a tint of red. "Chez. I've never..."

"I know." He interrupted me and placed a finger over my lips. "You've never been fucked and you've never turned."

What did he mean by turned?

I sat on the table and he held the back of my neck. His strong fingers raised my dress up past my thighs. He stared into my eyes intently and reached down to massage my clit *over my silk underwear. I began to groan and close my eyes.*

"Hey, look at me. I want you to look into my eyes while I do this, baby." He took his thumb and began making circles on my clit. I moaned. "Chez, please." I couldn't get the right words out. Our eyes were locked. The red inside of me wanted him to keep going, but I couldn't let it take over me. My body was betraying me.

He slid my underwear down and raised my dress above my breasts. He suckled my nipples making them hard. I swayed my head from side to side enjoying the feeling.

"Pen." He kept his lips close to my ear while he palmed my sex and I began to say his name. "Yes, baby. Say my fucking name. I own all of you." He grabbed my hair and pulled my body in close. I couldn't take it.

"Chez..." My eyes began to see red. I didn't stop him.

"We can start slow. I told you I can fuck you any way you want. I can fuck you the way he won't." He kissed my neck. Was he talking about Ford? Suddenly, the red in my eyes subsided.

I let go of Chez's hand. His fantasy disappeared.

"No!" I yelled.

Chez looked at me longingly.

"Penelope." He looked disappointed. "Why are you fighting the darkness?" He gave me another grin. "If that's your choice, then you *must* leave. Before it comes out of me. I don't want to kill you. Hell, maybe it's you that can kill me." He laughed. "That ruby magic...it's in you. You can turn into *it*."

Within seconds, he was thrown against the wall with a forceful electric green charge. He rose up and let out a raging howl. Flexing his entire body I could see red coursing through his veins. His abs were defined in the shadows, his arms swelled around him. He looked back at me and licked his lips.

"Chez!" Ford appeared growling, "What the hell did you do to her?"

He rushed over to me and shielded me. He was full of rage. Green pulses emanated from every single part of his body.

Chez began to laugh. "Ha. Ford. I didn't do anything but show her what she could have...what you won't give her. But I can. I saved her."

Ford inhaled and let out a loud howl. "Don't you fucking touch her, ever again. Even in your fantasies." Ford's eyes were piercing.

Chez began to build his power in his hands.

"Chez! Please! Don't." I begged. "We'll go. I'm sorry." I grabbed Ford's hand and his energy coursed through my veins. I felt the darkness in me diminish.

"Ford. Let's go." He wouldn't budge. "Please!"

"You've dug your own grave, Chez." Ford threatened.

He took my hand and in one second we were transported back to his house.

Ford stood in front of me staring at me, finally letting out a loud roar, "Damn it Penelope! He found you. Did he touch you? I could fucking kill him!" Ford gripped his hands together and darted for the bedroom.

He came back with his shirt off and started to dial someone on his phone. His body was strong and powerful.

I couldn't help but stare. His biceps flexed as he pulled out a cup to make tea for me. His dark hair was wet from the earlier rain. His eyes were resting on the stove waiting for the fire to light up. He was on the phone with his father, Winsten. After a few minutes he hung up and looked at me. I was still in slight shock and couldn't speak.

Ford walked over to me. "I'm dying here, Penelope? What happened? I need to know!"

I nodded my head and began to tell him what happened last night.

"Penelope. I'm so sorry. I should've been there! I should've protected you!" Ford yelled.

"Ford. Ford. It's okay. I'm okay. See, no blood." He wasn't amused and still seemed angry. He leaned closer to me and put his arms around my waist. He gazed at me. "Why did you do this? Why did you go looking for Sam without me? You could've died! Instead, Chez saved you. Chez found you!" Ford started to breathe hard.

"I know. I'm sorry. I couldn't sit around waiting for answers. I thought I could follow the elevator and find what I was looking for. Instead, I saw things I shouldn't have seen.

Ford, you should have seen those bodies. They were suspended in some sort of liquid energy. It was pink! Like mine..." I felt a tinge of fear come over me. Ford hugged me. I didn't want to tell him I had seen myself with Ruby magic, and that magic answered to Chez. I didn't know what to make of it, and I didn't know what to make of what Chez said about *turning*.

"Let me ask you one more time. Do you trust me?" he asked as he lifted me up from the couch and carried me to his bedroom.

"Yes. Ford. I always have. Sometimes I get frustrated when you don't tell me what is going on but, yes, I do trust you."

He laid me down on his bed, took hold of the red dress and began to raise it above my knees. He placed his hands on my thighs and rubbed them. I tilted my head back and closed my eyes.

"Penelope. Your smell. It's intoxicating." He slowly moved his hand up my inner-thigh. My body was responding. It was longing. Ford reached under his bed and pulled out a pair of handcuffs. I smiled.

He sat me up and put the handcuffs on me with my hands restrained behind my back. He reached in his top drawer and took out a knife. My eyes widened and I held my breath. He took the knife and started to cut my dress from the top to the bottom. My breasts were exposed. He ran his hands over my nipples and tugged them gently, putting his lips to my mouth and kissing me.

"Penelope. You wanted to be mine. I'll make you mine. Forever." He pulled the dress from underneath me and threw it across the room.

My inner essence was burning with desire.

I watched as his biceps protruded as he held himself up over my body. He leaned down and slowly kissed his way up my thighs. His soft lips made their way up towards my labia. Chills went down my spine and I arched my back to meet his touch. He slowly pulled my underwear over and started to gently lick my clitoris. I moaned. He was extremely good. He ran his hands up to my nipples once more and flicked them until they were erect. He slid my underwear off, first with his fingers then finished taking them off with his mouth. My wetness was dripping out of me as he took two fingers and guided them over my clit and made circles. I hated I was so new to this. But I was getting close to an orgasm and wanted to enjoy this even more. "Not yet, beautiful." Ford whispered in my ear. He moved his fingers and eased them around my labia. My mouth opened and I lost my breath. "Are you okay? Is this okay?" Ford whispered. I winced. My pink energy started emanating from my hands and feet. He looked at me pleased.

"It's okay. Relax." Ford looked at me.

I was turned on by his words and his dominance. My hands still handcuffed behind my back, Ford licked his fingers and unbuttoned his jeans. He let his erection free. I gasped. How painful was that going to be? I was biting my lip. I was waiting, nervous with desire.

"Are you sure, Penelope? He put his hand to my cheek."

"Yes." I begged.

"I want to take you with my tongue. Your scent, your taste, I want it all over me." Ford put his thumb on my clitoris while he tongued me. He was getting off on pleasing me, and I could feel his erection in between my legs. His green pulse was rampant. I was enjoying it with low moans.

"Penelope. You're perfect." He examined my entire body with his eyes.

He slid his erection and massaged my labia with it. My hands wanted to hold him, to put my arms around him, to dig my nails into him.

"I like seeing you longing for me, Penelope. I want to make sure you are okay with this. Especially if I'm making you mine." I nodded. He kissed my lips and pulled my hair back. I circled my hips. He took a condom and started to open it.

"Penelope...I want to make sure we are safe. As well, we still don't understand what your power and mine can do when we are together." Ford answered.

He leaned forward, began to kiss me again, and pressed his erection up to my clit. He gently spread my legs further apart and slowly eased himself inside me. I let out a painful moan muffled by his lips. "Shhh." He slowly pushed his erection in and out of me. His mouth still muffling my cries of pleasure. I could feel his soft skin against my face as he sucked my lips dry. Each time he entered me, I felt a small piercing pain, but it felt so good.

"God, you're so tight. Penelope, breathe." Ford said in short breaths. His body was pulsing green and I could see it flow throughout my body. I could feel his energy sucking me in. He released my hands from behind my back.

"Penelope, are you okay?" He asked.

A power was building in me. "I'm okay." I replied out of breath. He kept thrusting harder and harder each time. I could feel my wetness make it easier for him to slide in and out, or was that blood?

"Penelope. You're mine. This will always be mine." He looked at me as he made love to me with intensity. His hands stroking every part of my body. From my hair, to my stomach, down to my thighs, and beyond.

"Ford." I breathed heavily and put my hands on his shoulders. My legs tried to wrap around him, but I wasn't sure if that's where they should go.

He took a deep breath and moaned. "Penelope, your tightness..." Sliding in and out of me, he looked me in the eyes and moved his hand down over my clitoris and began to massage it. I was bursting at the seams, lost in pleasure. I couldn't contain myself, and the darkness that had been inside me was nowhere to be found.

"This is perfect. I'm your first and your last." He thrust harder and I yelped. I moaned and began to scream his name. "That's right, beautiful." He breathed in my ear. I put my arms around his neck.

"Come for me. I want to feel your orgasm on my erection. I want to feel what's mine," Ford said to me as he held me close.

Ford's body was a heavy green and his charge surrounded us. It began to suck the life out of me, and my body suddenly released a bright pink aura. As I unraveled all over him my energy burst out into electric pulses all over the room. Ford began to explode and breathe heavily. His green pulses devoured me, but my charge was too strong. It neutralized his and a white beam shot out and dissipated in the air.

I was still breathing heavily. Ford's breathing was heavy as he hovered over me, looking at me with intense eyes. He lifted himself from inside of me and moved to the bathroom. He came back with a small towel. I looked down and could see a tinge of pink on his sheets. He smiled at me. He took the towel that was soaked in warm water and started to clean me. I hesitated, but then let him, and instead laid thinking about what had just happened.

"You didn't kill me." I finally let out with a grin.

"I know..." he squinted.

"Maybe you are no match," I teased.

He smiled and handed me a shirt of his. I put it on and moved off the bed. He grabbed the sheets and threw them in the laundry room. "I'll have my maid come over later."

A maid? He had a maid?

He walked over to me and put his hands on my cheeks and raised my face. He kissed me passionately and led me to the couch.

"Penelope. I don't want you going out on your own anymore. Ever. I want to make sure I'm always with you. There are still so many things you need to learn, and now that Chez knows you exist, he will not stop until...you're his." Ford gritted his teeth and became angry.

"I will never be his," I answered.

"I know. I will never let it happen." He composed himself. "Come on. I'm going to take you home, unless you want to stay here."

"If it's okay with you, I rather stay here. It feels safer than my dorm," I said shyly.

"Yes, of course. I'll make a new bed. Drink some tea, and try and relax." He smiled at me and walked towards his bedroom.

I drank some tea and lay on the couch thinking about Chez, about what had just happened with Ford, about those bodies in the lab. Those people...

Chapter 13 – Harness

I awoke, remembering feeling super tired last night, and that I had fallen asleep in Ford's room. It felt like the middle of the night because it was still pitch black. I began to move around and get comfortable in Ford's bed, when I was aware of fingers gently traversing across my stomach. I felt the cold against my bare skin. A hand stroked my breasts and massaged my shoulders. I groaned "Ford..." as he went lower and slid off my underwear. His fingers crossed over my sex and I felt movement underneath the covers. "Ford, don't stop."

I felt a vibrating sensation. It hovered under the sheets, and then made its way to my inner thigh, slowly moving upwards. My eyes were shut and my back was arched. I could feel the tantalizing vibrator inserted into me.

"Oh God! What are you doing?" I yelped.

He licked my belly button with his sharp tongue while the vibrating sensation moved throughout my lower body. My hips flowed freely and I wanted so much more. I wanted his tongue on me, his hands on me, and his erection inside of me. I tried to reach down to grab his hair when I felt one of his hands pin my arms back, and the other pull my hair. My energy began to build inside of me.

"I don't know if I can take this, Ford." Just then, I felt a sensation around my back. I wasn't sure what was about to happen, but I was so lost in pleasure that I didn't object. I felt him slide a finger into me. I moaned and moved my hips in circles. He slid his finger in and out and took the vibrator and placed it on my clitoris. I begged him to take me.

No sooner had I begged him to keep going than he flipped me around and slid the vibrator into my butt. He grabbed my breasts sharply and I yelped. As I yelped he shoved his massive erection inside of my sex. Holy cow, he felt extremely erect and big. His thickness made me gasp for air. It hurt so badly, but I couldn't deny how good the pain felt. As he took me from behind, he raised me up with one hand tightly over my mouth and the other over my clitoris while he rammed himself into me. I breathed fast and heavy.

"What are you doing to me...don't stop." I pleaded.

It felt amazing, like nothing ever before. His erection filled me, and the vibrator only intensified the feeling. His strong hands gripped my breasts and massaged them for seconds before he licked his fingers and smacked my clit. Immediately he started to draw circles all over my clitoris. I tried to break free, but he held me with his massive arms. I was about to come. I was close. My energy was emanating. Emanating...red...but before I could come up with an answer I started to unravel all over him.

As I came he whispered in my ear. "This is how I would fuck you, This is how you deserve to be taken. You want more and I told you baby, I could give you that. Give in to me. You feel this, that's you all over me. And this..." He took the vibrator out of me "your pleasure." He took his hand off my mouth and I turned around. Towering over me was the powerful, muscular, mysterious Chez glowing the brightest red I could see.

"Ahhh!" I screamed. I sat up in bed.

"Pen! Pen! Are you okay? What's wrong!?"

I looked over at Ford sitting next to me. I grabbed my face and my hair and looked under the sheets. "It was just a dream, just a dream. Okay...okay." I composed myself. My breathing was erratic. I looked under the sheets again and saw a wet spot. Oh God, had I orgasmed in my sleep? To Chez? That was impossible but it felt so real.

"Pen, what's wrong?" Ford asked. He took me in his arms and hugged me close. I stayed silent. There was no way I was going to tell him what I had just experienced. It was only a dream but it felt excruciatingly real. I lay back down and stared into the darkness until I fell asleep again.

I had only been asleep for about an hour when a faint whisper woke me up, "Penelope." I opened my eyes and sat up quickly. The room was dark, but I could see Ford still sleeping next to me. I got out of bed and walked towards the window. I could see a faint red light outside. In that moment I heard a familiar squawk that startled me. It was Creed. I turned back to look at Ford, but he was still sleeping. Could he not hear what I had just heard? Did Creed waken me? Was his the voice I had heard in my head? I put my hand against the window and Creed lowered his head in acknowledgment.

"Penelope. Come."

Was that him talking to me? It had to be. Was I reading his mind? How did Creed end up here? How did he know where I was? So many questions I needed answers for, and maybe if this was real he would be the one to help me. I grabbed the red silk dress Chez had given me and tiptoed out the bedroom door. I wish I had something else to wear, but I had no time to worry about that now.

I walked towards the front door hoping Ford didn't have some alarm I didn't know about. As soon as I walked out, Creed, in all of his majestic glory, slowly walked towards me. I wasn't sure what was happening, but I knew he had called me. Creed put his head down so I could climb on top of him. I was hesitant, but hoisted myself onto his neck.

"Creed where are you taking me?" I said to him in my thoughts. *"You'll see,"* he responded. A smile came over me and with a lift of his great wings we were gone.

We flew through the darkness with amazing speed. I had no idea where we were going, but I felt safe with Creed, a huge Brindle that I just so happened to be able to communicate with and, well, he liked me. No sooner had we left Ford's house in the woods than we started to descend to the roof of the school's library. Oh, no! I thought. There was no way in hell I wanted to be around here. I clung to Creed for dear life as we descended.

"Creed. NO." I yelled as he eased me off his back. It was dark, the campus was eerie, and I wasn't going anywhere near that lab without Ford. Creed looked at me and put his forehead to mine.

"*My one. She is in there*" I could hear him say.

"Wait, your *one*?" I asked him in my thoughts.

Creed closed his eyes "*When you were here a few days ago, you unlocked someone very important to me. You saw her, and I could hear her through you. She was my partner in the battle of the Neons and Temulus. The Temulus took her captive and have been hiding her all these years. Us Brindles were the most sought after animals when Temulus and Neons went to war over power and territory. The Temulus tried to use us as conduits to control Neon energy. We possess natural powers of healing, rebirth, and eternal life. The Temulus have never stopped hunting us. When they took 'my one' I disappeared knowing I couldn't be captured if I were to save her. It's been years, but through you I finally know she's alive."*

I looked at Creed with tears in my eyes. "What am I supposed to do? She is trapped. I don't know what you want me to do." I said frustrated.

Creed looked at me in sadness and despair.

What was I supposed to do? Go back in that crazy lab and try to set her free? I was hesitant, and a wave of fear came over me thinking about those bodies. Ford explicitly told me not to do things like this without him, but Creed needed my help.

"Penelope. You are special. I'm your spirit guide in this world. This will sound unbelievable, but your mom told me to take care of you and protect you. The power that you have as a Brindle, our ability to communicate through our thoughts can become even more powerful when our energies unite. They say that only those chosen to imprint with a Brindle will be heavily rewarded throughout their lifetime. That's why I came to you."

My eyes widened when I heard his thoughts. My mom...I thought. What would she do? This Brindle knew my mom, but how? Maybe that is what Mara was trying to tell me all along, that my mother was also a Neon. Why had I never known about this before? Never in my whole life had I ever imagined that my mom was anything other than a regular wife and mother whose whole world was wrapped up in me and my dad. If I felt confused before, now I was doubly so.

"Creed, are you telling me you knew my mother?" I smiled.

He nodded and laid his head on the ground and I could hear him again. *"Yes, I did. Your mother was one of the most valiant warriors I had ever known."*

My eyes began to water thinking that the memories I had about my mother were not completely accurate, but I was happy that I was learning who she really was. She was a warrior and a beautiful woman. Creed kept on, *"I loved your mother very much. Her and I were connected just like you and me. Her energy fed my energy and we both had a great unity of power. She never wanted anyone to uncover the secret of eternal life, so she tucked it away within her-*

self so no one would know. The Temulus knew we could heal anyone or anything, but only theorized about us being able to give someone eternal life. During the war, your mother drew me away and used every last bit of her Neon power to extract the power of eternal life from me. She created an orb sphere with it and absorbed it into her body. She was pregnant at the time, Penelope. After that, she left and we never saw her again."

I put my hand on Creed's forehead and felt a charge run through me. "I'm going to help you." I said.

Creed stood up and stretched out his wings as far as they could go. A green energy flowed from the tips of his wings down to my hands. I felt powerful and extremely alert. While Creed waited outside, I made my way inside the library, to the elevator, and down to the lab. When the doors flew open, it was dark. The hospital lab was completely torn apart with cables all over the place. I began to think of the four pillars. If I could just get some light in here. My hands began to light up pink, and I could finally see what was in front of me. There was nothing there. My mouth fell open, and I ran down the hallways. What happened? Where were the rooms, the bodies, and the glass abyss where I had seen the other Brindle? It was as if none of it had ever existed. I ran towards the lab opening and everything was GONE. How could this be? I ran back out and could see Creed already knew what I had seen. He laid his head down in dismay.

"Creed, I'm sorry. We will find her, I promise. I will help you." I climbed on his neck and just as we were about to fly away, I heard a voice.

"Pen, baby." It was the same voice I had heard at Ford's. I thought it had been Creed. I lowered myself onto the ground and began to look around. Where was this voice coming from, and why was I drawn to it? I looked back at Creed and let him know that I would be okay walking back to my dorm. I needed to get back to some kind of normalcy. I opened the door to my room and I could see Velaire fast asleep in her bed. I tried not to make too much noise so as not to wake her up and have her yell and scream. I had been missing for a few days already, and I'm sure everyone was wondering where I was. No sooner I had slipped into bed than I heard Vel squeal and jump out of her bed.

"Pen! Where have you been? Holy shit you are back! We've been looking everywhere for you! Ronnie even called your dad!"

"Oh, no." I made my way towards the door.

"Wait, where are you going?" Vel asked as she hugged me tightly.

"I have to go find Ronnie. I have to call my dad. I think I lost my cell phone in all of this commotion." I started towards the door.

"Pen, wait! What commotion? You didn't even tell me what happened to you the last few days. Where were you? Were you with Ford...did you meet someone?" Vel looked at me with an eerie smile. It was as if she knew something. I slowly walked away.

"Um, yeah, I was with Ford. Sorry I didn't let you guys know." I looked at her confused face. "I need to go find Ronnie."

I ran out of the room and headed towards Ronnie's building. What day was it? I hadn't even been worried about my friends or family. When I got to Ronnie's dorm room I knocked quietly as I imagined he was asleep. He immediately opened the door.

"Penelope!" He screamed and threw his arms around me. I could feel his grip tighten as he towered over me. "Oh my God, where have you been? I've been worried. I called your dad. He said he was calling the cops! We couldn't find you! Where did you go?!" I slowly released myself from his grip and asked to borrow his phone so I could call my dad. On the third ring he picked up.

"Ronnie?" He answered.

"No." I looked over at Ronnie. "It's me." And with that he burst into tears and started to weep over the phone.

"I'm fine. I'm okay. I've just been with a new friend. His name is Ford."

Ronnie looked disappointed.

"I was with Ford. He wanted me to meet his parents, Mara and Winsten."

Dad was silent.

"I know," were the next words I could think of to break the silence. I could hear Guy let out a big sigh. "I'm okay and I think we have a lot to talk about." I hung up the phone as Ronnie looked at me, confused and worried.

"Pen, you were with Ford? What the hell! You couldn't pick up the phone and tell me that, better yet respond to my texts I've been sending you the last couple of days?"

"Ronnie, I lost my phone, I don't know what happened to it." I was worried about Ronnie's reaction. I was worried about how he was taking this.

"Pen, we looked everywhere for you. Lyla and I were so worried. Have you gone to see her yet? She's been crying her eyes out for the last two days!"

"No, Ronnie, I haven't." I held my breath. "I will find her in the morning. I just wanted to make sure you were okay." I could see Ronnie's worried face, but something about his response was different. I put my arm on his bicep and gave him a reaffirming look. As I slid my hand off his arm he reached out to grab it.

"Pen...I hope you know you scared me to death. I was completely lost the last two days not knowing where you were, and whether something might have happened to you. I couldn't imagine you being in danger and not being able to save you or take care of you. Honestly, I don't know if I can do this anymore. I'm just trying to have a good first year with my two best friends, and you keep leaving me in the dark." I looked at Ronnie with my eyebrows furrowed. Where was all this coming from? He was genuinely worried, but I sensed something else.

"Ronnie, I know, I am so sorry." I looked the other way.

"Look, I get it. You and I have been friends for a long time and you want someone who is going to just be your friend without asking any questions. Pen, I'm not that guy. I can't just stand here and watch while you throw part of your life away because some dude named Ford decided to show up." Ronnie said exasperated.

"You're right." I agreed. "Fine, I'll just leave you out of all of this. You won't need to deal with it." I was tired of him demanding so many answers from me. He was the one who had cheated all those years ago! And he wanted ME to be at his beck and call. Maybe it wasn't fair for me to hold his cheating over his head, but I needed something to keep my feelings at bay for all those years. I wasn't in love with him anymore, but part of me still held a small grudge.

I started to walk away.

"Pen, wait." He held my hand. "Please don't go. Can you come inside and just stay and hang out like old times?" I wasn't exactly sure how to respond, but something about the way he asked me seemed genuine and had a sense of normalcy, that I agreed. I was still in the Chez' red silk dress and felt extremely uncomfortable.

"Ronnie, do you mind if I borrow one of your shirts?" I asked.

"Of course not." Ronnie handed me an old Duke shirt he had purchased back in high school when my mom was still alive. In fact, he had worn this shirt to my birthday dinner right before my mom became sick.

"Thanks." I used his closet to change my clothes. I crumbled up the red dress and threw it in his trash bin. Something about being with Ronnie felt so normal.

"Ronnie, is it okay if I stay here?" I asked.

"Of course, you can stay on my bed and I'll stay on the couch." He motioned to the two seater next to his bed. His dorm room was rather big since his roommate had bailed, so naturally he had more space. I got into his bed and, no sooner than I had tucked myself in, I fell asleep.I was asleep for what seemed like three hours, and it probably was. I could hear voices in the hallway, Ronnie getting ready, and the sun was brightly shining through the windows of the room. Good God, what time was it? I felt like I had barely slept. I looked at Ronnie's alarm clock that read 7:00 am, Monday. Oh shit! Monday? Monday, already? My first day of class was today. I hadn't given my schedule much thought, but I knew my first introductory class started at 8:00am.

"Ronnie!" I was startled.

"Morning sleepy head." He responded.

"I'm going to be late! Why didn't you wake me up? I don't even know where my schedule is. I need to get ready and get dressed!" I yelled.

"Relax! I've got everything for you. Don't you remember, you and I picked all of the same classes before we got here? All I had to do was pick up your schedule. I just told them I was your brother and they believed me. Strict security, huh?" Ronnie laughed. He wore jeans and a Duke hoodie for his first day. "Also, I woke up early and headed to your dorm to pick up some clothes for you. Vel was awake and was able to open the door for me. She's a strange girl, you know?" He looked at me with one eyebrow raised.

"Don't I know it?" I responded.

"Let me call Lyla and tell her to meet us outside my dorm, and we can figure out how we get to these classes." Ronnie started to phone Lyla. As soon as she picked up, and Ronnie told her where I was, I could hear her loud screams through the phone. At first they sounded happy and then they turned into anger and some cuss words. Great, she was definitely going to be mad at me.

Ronnie gave me the keys to the bathroom, so I could clean up and get ready for class. As I walked back to Ronnie's dorm room, I could see Lyla waiting by the open door. She looked at me with anger and dismay, but then a smile came to her face and she ran towards me and lunged at me with a gigantic hug.

"Pen! What the hell were you thinking? You were with Ford this whole time? Are you crazy? Ronnie just told me all about it. I can't believe you didn't tell me. Where is your phone? Did you not see the millions of text messages I sent you?"

"No." I answered her with a reassuring look. "I'm sorry" I managed to get out.

"It's all right. I just want you to tell me when you go sneak off with Ford. That is highly unlike you. Oh my God, wait. Pen. Please don't tell me you and him..." She motioned her two fingers together.

"What!" I exclaimed. "No!" I yelled. Ronnie was standing right next to us as she asked me. I couldn't tell her anything about what had happened with Ronnie in our midst. In fact, I couldn't really tell anyone about anything.

I still wasn't ready to head to class.

"I forgot my books and my phone. I need to go to my dorm and get them." I told Ronnie. Both Lyla and Ronnie followed closely behind. When I got there Vel wasn't there and her bed was made. I guess she had gone to class herself. I grabbed my books and walked out the door. Ronnie, Lyla, and I started our walk to class. I wondered where my cell phone had gone. My guess is it was lost in between me getting frustrated with Ford, finding dead bodies in a lab, and getting abducted by Chez.

We got to our first class and sat down. The class was small, but was held in a rather large classroom. Our professor was old, of course. He wore a nice suit, reader's glasses, and was probably as tall as me. He was a short guy with really pronounced lips and an impressive vocabulary. This was going to be an interesting semester.

"Ronnie, can I borrow your phone?" I whispered.

"Sure." He handed it to me.

I figured I could call my phone and see if someone had picked it up or possibly use my find phone feature. I stepped out of class into the hallway and dialed my number. It rang only once and sounded like someone had picked up, but there was only silence.

"Hello?" I asked. I could hear a familiar breathing.

"Pen. Sweet angel." The voice responded.

"Who is this? Why do you have my phone?" I answered impatiently.

"Baby, it's Chez. Don't hang up."

I started to pace and a million thoughts ran through my head about the events that transpired over the last few days.

"Pen, I know how important your phone is to you. It's full of videos and pictures of your mother and, if I had to guess, it's the only place where you have these stored. Also, a little birdie told me you were around Sam's lab last night looking for someone or something…"

I could sense his smile through the phone. A tear rolled down my cheek. "You asshole!" I whispered into the phone.

"I'm going to text you a location. Write it down then delete it. If you want your phone back, meet me there tonight at 9:00 pm. Otherwise, you'll never get it back, or any of these precious memories. You should really think about saving these images elsewhere. One click of a button and I can delete your whole life."

"Don't you dare! Tell me where the Brindle is!" I yelled at him.

"Oh yes, Reya. Such a beautiful creature. Maybe, if you show up, I will let you in on where she is."

He hung up.

I was furious! I couldn't focus. Not only did he have any remaining memories of my mother in his hands, but he knew where Reya was! The most important being in Creed's life had such a beautiful name. I was going to help Creed, and find out where she was being held captive. Seconds later I received a text message with a location on a map. I zoomed in on the map. I was surprised. He had texted me the location of The Port. There was no way I was going there again, but if I wanted the only known surviving memories of my mother, I had no choice. I deleted the text and headed back towards class. I handed Ronnie his phone and sat down. Unable to concentrate or focus, I put my earphones in and listened to music. I couldn't bear to listen to this teacher, and couldn't stop thinking about Chez and my phone.

Chapter 14 – Rescue

As soon as class was over I rushed back to my dorm. I needed to arm myself, to think about what was going to happen in the next few hours meeting up with Chez. I wasn't about to say a word about this to Ford. As soon as I finished showering and made my way back to my room I saw Vel sitting on her bed reading a book. She seemed to be wrapped up with something because she didn't even bother to look up at me as I came in. I put on some jeans, a red shirt, and my white flats and sat in the middle of my bed just thinking. So many things going through my head.

"Vel, don't wait up for me later. I have some studying to do, and I let Ford know I'd be meeting up with him at some point."

Vel put her book down. "Penelope, are you sure you are going to be okay? I just want to make sure you are going to be safe."

"Yes, I'll be fine" I half smiled.

"Okay, well, you have no phone, so how are we supposed to get a hold of you if we need to?"

I looked at her in dismay. "I'll get another one when I'm out but, for now, I will be okay." I grabbed my hoodie from the chair and threw it on.

I didn't want to go to The Port alone. I wasn't sure what I would find, plus I had to keep it all a secret. One thing I hadn't thought of—how was I going to get there? I couldn't get anyone to go with me. Who could I get to take me there and still keep my secret? I didn't want to think about it, but maybe Sarina was my only option. She was a Neon, and the last time we had an encounter, she tried to get me to "be" with her. I had saved her life with the Cloaks, and Ford looked after her after that big mess in the theater. I rolled my eyes and started out the door. If I was going to find Sarina, I had to talk to Malee. I wondered how that would go. I hadn't seen Malee since I tried to kill her. Well, more accurately, since my rage had tried to kill her. There were so many unexplained things, and I didn't feel like I was getting many answers from Ford. Maybe meeting with Chez was a good thing. I'm sure he wanted to kill me too, but at least he was more apt to tell me the truth, or so I thought given his savage carelessness.

I left the room and started to walk towards Malee's house. As soon as I got there, I could see the lights were on, and there was definitely some activity inside. I held my breath and knocked on the door. The door opened and there was Malee. She looked at me with terror, and she looked like she had not been to school today. Her eyes were sunken in, her hair was a mess, she was pale, and her t-shirt and sweatpants looked crumpled.

"What are you doing here?" She immediately spoke. I could hear the angst in her voice.

I stumbled, "I...I was hoping. Well, I wanted to…". Damn it! I couldn't get the right words out. I had to tell her I was sorry, I had almost killed the girl!

"Malee, can I come in?" She looked at me in confusion. She opened the door wider and stepped aside. I walked in and sat down on her leather couch in the living room.

"Malee, look, I have no idea what happened to me that night. I don't know what came over me."

She still hadn't said a word.

"I'm really sorry. I don't know if Ford explained any-thing to you."

"No." She interrupted me. "Ford didn't tell me anything at all. I haven't seen him since, well, what you did." A tear began to roll down her face. I was both relieved and sad.

"Malee, I never meant to hurt you. There is something wrong with me, and I hope one day I can explain it all. I came to say I was sorry but also, I need to find Sarina."

Malee furrowed her eyebrows. "Sarina? For what?"

"I need her to take me to The Port. Please help me." I gave her a brief look. "Please."

Malee grabbed her phone and started to dial a number.

"Thank you so much. This means a lot to me." I half smiled.

"Ford told me what happened that night. What you did…and why you did it. I feel sorry for you, Penelope." Malee said in a soft tone.

I looked at her with sadness in my eyes. I couldn't respond.

We waited about 10 minutes and then we heard a car roaring outside of Malee's apartment. She motioned me out the front door.

"Thank you, Malee." I locked eyes on her with sincerity, and then rushed out the door.

In a red Camaro, wearing a red dress, and with her long red hair, Sarina motioned me over.

"Pen, Malee said you wanted to find me. What's the deal, Penny?" She smiled coyly.

"Sarina, can you take me to The Port? I don't have a car or a phone, and I need to meet someone there." Where the hell did she get off calling me Penny anyway?

She raised her eyebrows and looked at me inquisitively.

"Get in." She responded.

We drove most of the way in silence up until the last five minutes.

"So, does Ford know you are meeting with Chez?" She turned to look at me with a smirk.

"What? No! How did you know?" I was surprised.

"Pen, I know a lot of things you may not know. For someone who also has Neon abilities, you should know I'm pretty in tune to a lot of things." She laughed wryly. I looked at her for a minute. So she was a Neon. Ford must have known when she had made me think those crazy thoughts when I ran into her at that party.

"Chez has my phone. I need it back." I answered.

"Your phone? Well, whatever is on it must be pretty important if you're willing to meet with the angel of darkness at a club where mostly Neons go. I take it Ford doesn't know. I would be careful if I were you." She unlocked my door.

She considered Chez an angel? I wouldn't think he'd be an angel of anything! Part of me wanted her to stay. I was afraid, but also needed to find out if I could do this on my own.

"Let me know when you need a ride home. Get your phone back, and call me. I'll come get you, Penny." She smiled.

"Can you please not call me Penny? And yes, I'll call you later. Thank you." I shut the door and walked towards the front door of the bar.

There was a bouncer at the door and an actual line of about twenty people. I stood at the back of the line.

"You. Over here." The bouncer motioned for me to step out of line and come to the front. I looked at him confused and walked towards him. He unclipped the velvet rope and directed me to walk inside. I handed my hoodie to the girl at the door and realized that tonight I may have been somewhat underdressed. I didn't care. All I wanted was my phone and to go home.

As soon as I entered there were two men with suits at the entrance to the dance floor. They stared at me and followed my every move with their eyes. I acted nonplussed and walked towards the bar to get some water. The place was crowded. I could barely get through all the people dancing and drinking the night away. The two men in suits walked closer to me and stood on the other side of the bar watching me intently. I was definitely not in the proper attire for this night's festivities. Everyone looked beautiful and straight out of a Vogue magazine. I kept looking around to try and find Chez. How was I supposed to find him in this sea of people? What seemed like twenty minutes went by. I thought at this point I might as well order a drink. I ordered a whiskey with soda as it was the only thing I ever drank with my "dad".

I finished one drink, then two. I was getting a little impatient waiting on Chez. Where was he? I decided I would at least try and have fun while I waited for this egomaniac. I grabbed another drink and started towards the dance floor. I wasn't one for attention or solo entertainment,but the drinks were definitely playing a part in my carelessness. At this point, with so many things going on, and my life flipped upside down, what did I care! I danced for about five minutes when I felt someone rub up against me. I quickly turned around to see a guy trying to dance with me. "Hey, baby, I like your style. Dance with me." He grabbed me by the waist.

"No." I immediately slapped his hand away.

"Oh come on, I'm what's on the menu for you tonight. A little dancing isn't going to hurt you. You look like you're all alone tonight." He proceeded to grab my lower back.

I was about to let him have it when I felt an arm grab mine and pull me away.

"She said NO. Could you not hear her over the loud music, or were you just choosing to be a stupid?" It was Chez. He shielded me with his body. He was dressed in all black and I could feel his muscles protruding from his shirt as he held me behind him.

"Sorry, I didn't mean to cause issues." The guy quickly made his way across the dance floor and to the bar.

"Chez." I faintly let out. He was towering over me with intense eyes looking into mine. "Pen." He responded. We stared at each other for what seemed like 30 minutes, but turned out to be only seconds before he began to talk.

"So, you decided to actually meet me." He moved his lips very close to my ear. "I'm impressed, and you didn't bring anyone with you I see."

I wasn't going to mention Sarina, and I was frozen in my tracks hearing his voice. It brought back some strange and unwanted memories from my attack. I couldn't tell if it was the drinks or the high level of stress, but I felt the urge to vomit and I was about to faint. I looked at Chez while we stood on the dance floor and then my vision went black.

What seemed like a few minutes later, I awoke on a couch in a dark room with the scent of roses everywhere. What had happened? Had Chez set up a trap for me? One minute I was at the bar on the dance floor, the next I am in a dark room. I felt for my clothes and was relieved they were the same ones from earlier. Did I faint? God, my head was spinning. I could still hear loud music. Please tell me I'm trapped in a horrible dream. I sat up and looked for the nearest door. As soon as I started to get out of the bed, I heard him.

"Hi, baby. Whoa, whoa, whoa. Don't try and get up so fast. Relax." Chez spoke.

I squinted my eyes to try and see him in the shadows, but he wouldn't show himself.

"What did you do to me and where am I?" I began to ask impatiently.

"Pen, I did nothing. You drank too much and passed out on the dance floor. You were reckless." He chuckled. "I took you upstairs to a back room for VIPs, so you could regain your composure."

Why was he making me feel so stupid? Maybe I was a little reckless drinking so much. The loud music wasn't helping my headache.

"Where's my phone? Better yet, where is Reya!" I demanded.

"Shh, shh. That will be something we can talk about." He slyly responded.

"Why can I not see you? Why is it so dark in here?" I demanded answers.

"It's dark because I deem it to be dark. You can't see me, because I choose for you not to see me. I control the situation." Chez regained some force in his voice. I was getting tired of his stupid games. I just wanted my phone.

"I need to see you." I demanded. No sooner had I spoken than I saw two red eyes glow in the dark. I gasped.

"You requested it. You are seeing. Now what?"

"Damn it Chez! Tell me where Reya is, and give me my Goddamn phone and come out of the darkness. Or else…"

Within seconds Chez lunged at me and grabbed me by the neck and pinned me against the wall. I was running out of breath with small gasps.

"Or else what, sweet girl?" He roared. I stared in complete disbelief and shock as I witnessed the creature standing before me.

As he held me pinned up against the wall, I could see the moonlight shine upon his black wings. He had tattoos all over his body from his neck down to his waist. His eyes were a bright red color, and there was a pulse of red energy emanating from his hands.

"Chez," I chokingly responded. He let go some of his grip and put his lips close to my neck.

"I say when you get something, and when you don't. I say when you leave, and when you stay." He whispered and I could see his sharp teeth surround his salivating tongue. A tear rolled down my cheek, and I squinted as I tasted the saltiness. If there had ever been a time when I'd been scared of someone, it was happening right now.

"Don't cry, baby." He wiped a tear from my face with his thumb. I pulled my face away from his hands.

"You came here for your phone. I wanted to give it to you and let you leave, but when I saw you I just couldn't do it. You walked in and I couldn't help but think how beautiful you are. Your long dark hair, those eyes seeming to penetrate anyone they look at, and your toned body. Pen, I've been waiting for you for a long, long time." He stopped and smelled me, as if he smelled my fear.

"Chez, please. I don't have anything you want. I just want my phone. It's all I have of memories of my mother." I teared up again.

"Oh, Pen. Don't cry baby. Please." Chez took my phone and asked that I unlock it. He began to scroll through my pictures. "Where are these memories you speak of? Is it this photo album called My Heart?"

Chez opened the album and began to scroll. Suddenly, his entire demeanor changed. His wings folded away and disappeared, and his red energy dissipated. Chez handed me my phone. It was set on a picture of my mom as he huffed and roared.

"Go. Now!" He yelled. "Get the hell out!"

I grabbed my phone and ran out of the room. What? This didn't make sense. Why was he sending me away so suddenly? Was it my mom? What had happened? As I ran downstairs back towards the dance floor, I started to call Ford. As soon as I made it outside of the door, I saw his armored truck.

"Penelope! What were you doing?" He asked me in a direct tone.

"Ford!" I yelled as I jumped into his truck.

"Penelope, what's wrong?" He grabbed my face in his hands.

"Chez..." I began to speak.

"What! What do you mean Chez? Is he in there? I'm going to kill him. I told him to stay away from you!" Ford growled.

"Ford, don't! I went to Chez. I looked for him. He had my phone from when I was attacked and I wanted it back." I looked down.

He looked at me disappointed.

"Penelope. I told you not to do anything stupid or dangerous. Especially without me knowing!" He said forcefully.

"I'm sorry." I nodded my head. I knew what I had done was stupid, and I should have thought it through.

"Penelope, you don't understand what Chez is. You don't understand what he can do to you." Ford tried to explain.

"I know. I saw." I responded.

"What? You saw what?" Ford questioned me.

"I saw him...turn." I quietly whispered.

"You saw him turn?" Ford put his car in drive and fiercely drove down the long winding road to the dorms. He was quiet the whole way back to campus. His grip on the steering wheel was intense, and he hadn't taken his eyes off the road.

"Ford…" I quietly called out.

"What!" He yelled.

"What's wrong? Why are you so upset?" I asked.

"Penelope. You really don't know what you've gotten yourself into. I tell you to do one thing because it's for your own good, and you don't listen! All I'm trying to do is to protect you from everything, and you go and put yourself in harm's way. I don't get it!" He was anxious and upset.

"I'm sorry!" I yelled.

"Penelope. You want to know something? The Temulus are not like us. They are barbaric! They are monsters. You saw Chez turn because he has that evil Ruby magic in him. Ruby magic is what gives him that ability to transform into what he is." Ford couldn't stop his anger.

"Yes! So what! What the hell does that even mean!" I started to yell.

Ford slammed on the brakes in front of my dorm and put his truck in park. "It means he's branded you! A Temulus will only transform in front of a potential mate. A potential lover. A soul mate. Which means he thinks you are that!" Ford raised his voice. "He's trying to take your power away. You have Ruby magic. He wants it!" Ford exclaimed.

"But he didn't do anything to me. He let me go." I answered.

"Penelope, don't be so naive." Ford remarked.

"So I'm naive? Because I'm telling you what happened tonight, and I've shown that I can take care of myself? Where were you when I was attacked at the lab by Sam and that stupid doctor? I didn't see you come save me. You know who did? Chez did! He saved me and healed me!" I yelled.

Ford looked at me in dismay. "Penelope, please don't do this." He said quietly.

"Ford, no." I held my breath for a second. I looked over at him. "Ford, I don't care what Chez did, or if he branded me, or anything. I'm yours. That's how it will stay. That's how it will be. Thank you for driving me back. I'm tired and I've had a long night. Please, I'll call you in the morning." I opened the car door.

Ford took my face in his hands and kissed me passionately. "Okay." He whispered.

I walked towards my dorm room. With Velaire already asleep, I slipped into bed and drifted off to sleep.

Chapter 15 – Revelation

I awoke the next morning to the brightest sun I had seen in a long time, and a splitting headache. Why did I drink so much last night? It was ridiculous. I had a half-day of classes today that I wasn't even sure if I wanted to attend. I looked over to see Vel working on a painting. She had her headphones in, bopping her head around. I sat up in bed and motioned to get her attention.

"Pen! Morning!" She yelled.

"Hey. Do you have anything for a headache?" I asked.

Vel tossed over a pack of aspirin.

"Thank you." I took out two pills and started to chew on them.

"So, where the heck were you last night? I didn't go out that late, but you definitely weren't here." Vel asked.

"I was just out with Ford." I smiled.

"Just out with Ford? That's it?" She looked at me curiously.

"Yes. I'm going to get in the shower." I got up from bed and smirked at her.

I grabbed my towel and walked to the bathroom. I got to an empty shower and started to undress. I looked down at my legs and my hands. For some reason they looked rather pale. Maybe I was just dehydrated. I turned on the water and let the cold drops hit my face and body. I felt strange chills down my body. As the water turned hot I could see my breath in front of me. This didn't make sense. A dim red energy began to flow from my hands. I was startled and immediately began to look around for Chez. I didn't see anyone.

"Who else is in here?" My adrenaline began to drive me.

As I was grabbing my towel, Sarina slipped into the shower in front of me. "Hey." She smiled. "It's just me." She was completely naked. I looked at her in minor shock and proceeded to begin showering again. We stared at each other for a minute until she finally spoke.

"Well, don't let me stop you. I'm just trying to get clean, too." She started to lather her body.

I looked away but couldn't help watching her scrub her body. She was so perfect. How does someone look that perfect? She had an hourglass figure, perfect red hair, and her boobs. They looked fake. Were they? They were so round and full. Oh gosh! What was I doing? Why was I so enamored with her body? I didn't understand, but a feeling inside me was building. I looked back down at my hands. They were red, but why? Sarina rinsed her body and looked over at me with a smile. I gasped and held my breath. She moved closer to me, and her body pushed up against mine. As she moved in close she grabbed the shower handle.

"You really shouldn't keep the water this hot. It can damage your pretty hair, and your skin." She said as she turned the handle to the cold setting. Her mouth close to my cheek, and I could feel her breathing. She traced my arm from my shoulder down to my lower back. I started to breathe quickly. I couldn't really say anything. I didn't *want* to say anything. My only confusion was seeing a red aura from my body. As she traced my lower back with her fingers she leaned in and kissed my neck. Her kisses were so tender, her touch was so soft, and she felt good to the touch. I took her hand and looked at her with reservation. As soon as my hand touched hers the red energy consumed our bodies. I felt completely and utterly defenseless. She pushed me against the running water and began to kiss my neck and suck on my chest down to my nipples. I moaned and circled my hips.

"Penny, I didn't know, did you?" Sarina smiled.

It was like this red energy had a hold of me and I didn't want to let go. My hands grabbed her hips and pushed her away. She quickly lunged with more force and started to kiss me. I kissed her back with fervor. Her hand made its way to my sex and she started to circle my clitoris. My moaning intensified. Her lips never left mine. "Penny, let me help you. Let me help you unleash your desires." My head tilted back in pleasure. I was on the verge of an orgasm as she placed her lips over mine, and I felt a sudden power start to draw energy out of my body. I looked at her and could see red leaving my lips. I panicked and mustered all my energy to strike her with my pink aura. It seemed as if she was trying to suck out my energy, or was my energy pulsating because I was enjoying the feeling? I couldn't tell! Sarina fell against the shower wall and passed out. Oh no. What did I do! I grabbed my towel and wrapped her in it. I quickly put my clothes back on and tried to carry her to me room. I managed to make it to the room and threw the door open. Vel was still painting.

"Oh my God!" She yelled. "What is going on? Is that Sarina? What happened!" She was extremely nervous.

"Vel, calm down. She was in the shower and she slipped and fell," I said as I laid Sarina on my bed. "Look, I'm going to leave her here. I need to find Malee. Can you just please take care of her?" I begged. Vel nodded and started to get some of her clothes out of the closet.

I grabbed my phone and ran out of my dorm room. I kept running until I reached Ronnie's building. I felt as if I was having an anxiety attack, but fortunately Ronnie was leaving his dorm to go to class and saw me.

"Pen! Pen! My God!" He ran over to me and grabbed me in his arms. "Pen, what's wrong. Are you okay? What's going on?"

I was too weak to stand up. Ronnie lifted me up and carried me inside to his dorm room. I laid on his bed weeping until I was finally able to calm down. Ronnie sat next to me looking at me the entire time.

"Pen, let me help you." He moved my hair out of my face. "Pen, what's going on? Ever since we arrived on campus, you've been completely different. I never see you anymore. You don't talk to me or Lyla. We've tried for days to be with you and talk to you, and we never find you. You're always off with Ford, or on your own. Please talk to me and stop keeping me in the dark." Ronnie held my hands together.

I wordlessly looked up at him and stared off into the corner of the room.

"Okay, I will leave you alone to think, but I'm staying right here." Ronnie sighed.

Ronnie knew me well. I didn't want to talk. I didn't want to move. I just wanted to be. The last time he had seen me like this was when my mother died. Ronnie walked over to his mini fridge and took out a bottled water and put it next to me on the bed. He was distraught. His eyes were sad. I ended up falling asleep and missing my classes for the day. When I awoke Ronnie was still there reading a book.

"Ronnie, what time is it?" I sounded groggy.

Ronnie immediately sat up straight and came over to me. "Pen, you've been asleep for eight hours. It's close to 6:00pm." He smiled at me.

"Oh. Ugh, my head." I sat up and held my neck.

"Pen, don't move so much. Are you okay? What happened? Do you remember what happened this morning?" Ronnie was impatient.

"Yes, I remember." I nodded.

"What's going on then? Can you talk to me?" Ronnie asked.

"Ronnie, I can't. If I tell you, you will be in danger for knowing too much about me, about Ford. So much has happened in the last few weeks. I can't put you or Lyla in danger. When the time is right, you will know." I hesitated.

"You're my best friend. I hate keeping anything from you, but it's for your safety." Ronnie held my hands in his.

"Pen, I would do anything for you. Anything to keep you safe. Please, remember that." He kissed the top of my hand.

"Thank you, Ronnie. Hey, you want to go to dinner? You, Lyla, and me?" I looked at him with remorse.

Ronnie's eyes lit up. "Pen, yes! Let me call Lyla now."

While he dialed Lyla, my phone vibrated. I took it out of my pocket and saw Ford was calling. What was he calling for? I couldn't seem to get a break from anyone or anything. If it wasn't Ford, it was Chez, if it wasn't Chez, I had Sarina acting like a vulture. I was sick of it. I wanted normalcy. I wanted my friends. I ignored Ford's call and walked out of the dorm with Ronnie. We waited outside for Lyla. As soon as she saw me she came running to give me a hug. It felt so good to see her and have it just be us three again. We made our way down to dinner. At dinner, we had drinks, we had food, and we laughed the night away as if everything were normal again. I was having a great time catching up with my friends. I was happy for these precious few moments. My phone began to vibrate again. Who it was this time? I grabbed it out of my pocket. It was Guy. Guy? Why would he be calling me so late? I figured he caught my drift when I told him I knew he wasn't really my father. I ignored it, but he continued to call. I stood up from the table and walked to a corner of the restaurant.

"Hello, Guy?" I answered.

"Hi, Penelope." He paused for a moment. "I know it's late and I didn't want to call you like this, but it's my job to keep you safe whenever I can. There is trouble coming." He managed to get out.

Boy, if he knew what I had already been through. I'd say I had already gotten into plenty of trouble, and then some.

"I know. What is it?" I asked him hurriedly.

"It's Chez and the Temulus. They are getting ready to wage a war. Chez wants you. He wants the Ruby power you have inside of you. He has gotten close to you a few times I am told, but you have to know one thing. Chez can't have you or compel you to be with him, you have to go with him willingly, and he will stop at nothing until you do.

I went to see Winsten and Mara, and there is a lot of unrest in The Kingdom. Pen, Chez will stop at nothing until you're his. There have been visions of the Temulus attacking The Kingdom and killing every last Neon until you are one of them."

I started to hyperventilate. "Pen, are you there?" Guy kept asking.

"Yes." I took a loud gulp. "I'm here."

"Pen, I need you to take care of yourself. Please, stay close to Ford. You know, I'm sorry I never told you anything about all of this. About me. Please know, despite where you think you are right now, I have always loved you like my daughter. I cared for you and took care of you for most of your life. You are my family."

Tears rolled down my face.

"Guy, thank you. I have to go." I walked back to our table.

"Ronnie, Lyla. I have to go." I put some cash on the table and headed towards the parking lot.

"Pen! Wait!" Ronnie ran after me. "Pen, where are you going?"

"Ronnie, I need to find Ford. I have to do something." I responded.

"Of course. Ford. Pen, if you're going to keep me in the dark, at least do it without mentioning another guy's name." Ronnie sounded annoyed.

"Wait, what? What's your deal?" I became defensive.

"Pen! Don't you see it? Don't you see me?" Ronnie cried out.

"See what?" I was confused.

"Pen, I still love you!" Ronnie's eyes widened. As he finished his words I could hear footsteps come up behind me. I turned around to see Ford. With shock in my eyes and no words to say, Ronnie stared at me and nodded his head in disappointment. He began to walk away.

"Ronnie, wait!" I called after him, but he kept on walking.

"Penelope. How is it that you are so loved by everyone? This makes it harder for me." Ford pursed his lips. "Others want you."

"Yeah, well, you don't have to think about those others." I answered.

Ford stroked my cheek. "I came to find you. Guy called me and said he would try to get hold of you. There are bad things coming, and my priority is to keep you safe. The Temulus know all about you. Penelope, I'm not going to let anyone hurt you." Ford pulled me in close and began to kiss me. This was the touch I wanted to feel. The warm lips I wanted to taste. I let out a sigh of relief and then thought about Sarina. What would Ford say? I couldn't tell him. He had already thought Sarina was trying to go after my powers. Except, maybe he was right. We kissed for what seemed like a good while before we made it to his truck. As I climbed into his truck, I looked at his rearview mirror and could see Ronnie in the distance. He hung his head low and kept on walking.

"I want to take you home," Ford said. I smiled as he lifted me up into his truck, and we drove to his house. As Ford put his truck in park we could see something at his front door.

"Stay here," He commanded. Ford got out of his car and ran towards his front door and started to take his jacket off.

I immediately got out of the car and ran in his direction. There was a man, a Neon, laying on the ground at his front door. He was completely naked and covered in a thick liquid. The same liquid I had seen at the lab. His arms were full of holes and a note was tied to his neck.

Just one of many. I hope she's not losing control of her red. We'll see her soon.

Ford ripped up the note and let out a raging scream. It echoed throughout the woods.

"We have to take him to The Kingdom." Ford hoisted him up and grabbed my hands. He instantly transported us to the castle. Winsten and Mara rushed over as soon as they saw us.

"What happened to him?" Winsten took him from Ford and laid him down on a sofa.

"They left him on my front door with a note!" Ford growled.

"Who are *they*?" Mara asked.

"The Temulus." Winsten shook his head.

"Wait, how do you know these are Temulus?" I asked.

"They've done this before." Winsten confirmed. "Get him to our doctor, now! He is weak from the transport." He ordered two other Neons to carry him away.

"The Temulus have long been capturing Neons and ridding us of our powers, or experimenting on the weaker ones to wage warfare." Winsten sighed.

"Wait." I turned to look at Ford. "So then Sam, the bodies, the doctor. They are all working with the Temulus?" I cried out.

Ford nodded and placed his arms around me as I started to cry. Winsten and Mara looked at us with confusion.

"I hadn't told you, but Pen was captured by Sam. I had no idea. They almost took her power but she managed to escape. Before she did, she saw their lab. She saw all the Neon prisoners they had taken." Ford stroked my hair and hugged me. "It's okay, Pen. We will try and save them all." He comforted me.

"Penelope." Mara interrupted. "Go out to the garden, I think someone misses you." Mara took Winsten's hand and they headed back towards the corridor as Ford gave me a confused look. I ran towards the door and the outside fog.

Within seconds, I could feel the air created as immense wings flapped in front me and, I saw it was Creed.

He lowered his head and I reached out to hug him. In that moment I felt comfort, I felt a good strong connection. Our powers started to meld and our minds connected. In a sudden spur of thoughts, I could feel, see, and hear all of Creed's memories. I lay with him stunned, and in tune with his visions.

There was one memory with him as a baby and his mother. They were eating in a field. Seemed like a time before Brindles were held captive. His memory quickly shifted to him meeting Ford, Winsten, and Mara for the very first time. I could feel his grateful heart. The last memory slowly crept up from behind a huge cloud of smoke. As the smoke cleared, I saw Creed and next to him was another Brindle. They were in the middle of a war. I could see shots of fire flying across the air. There were explosions happening, and Creed was protecting the other Brindle under his wings. As the dust settled, Creed raised his wings to reveal a beautiful Brindle with a dark red hue. My heart dropped to the ground. It was the same Brindle I had seen in Sam's lab, it was Reya. In that moment, a dart shot through the air hitting the Brindle in the side of the neck. It let out a loud squawk and collapsed to the ground. I could hear Winsten ordering Creed to stand down and fly back towards the Neon army. The Temulus closed in on Creed and the Brindle, until Creed finally rose up and flew up into the sky. The red Brindle was dragged away.

I sat up from hugging Creed and tears rolled down both of our faces.

"Creed, I am so sorry," I sobbed. "I saw Reya."

Creed's eyes widened. "I saw her when I was attacked by Sam. He is someone working with the Temulus to somehow bring me into their army as their leader."

Creed whimpered and put his head next to mine.

"Creed, yes, I promise I will find her. I will do everything in my power to bring her back to you." I became angry. Creed lay down and I lay down next to him. Tonight I was not going to leave Creed's side.

Chapter 16 – Uprising

I awoke to the sound of Creed lapping water in a nearby reservoir. I stood up and walked towards him, but I began to get dizzy. My vision was becoming black and I felt as if I was going to faint. Creed rushed to me and let out a loud noise. I could see Ford throw the door open. "Penelope!" He yelled. I fell to my knees. Ford quickly picked me up and took me inside the castle. My vision and hearing was going in and out.

Winsten rushed inside the room. "Ford, the Temulus are here."

"How many?" Ford questioned.

"About 100. We need to gather the Neon army. They've come for her."

Those were the last words I heard before everything went black.

****

When I awoke I could hear explosions and yells coming from outside of my room. I ran to the door, but it was locked. I yelled out for anyone who could hear me but nothing worked. I thought for a minute and then began to harness the little power I knew I had. My hands began to glow pink and I ran towards the door. I was able to break the lock and open the door, and make my way to the front of the castle where I could see the Neons and the Temulus in a pitched battle. There were hundreds of them, but I couldn't see Ford anywhere.

I made my way outside, and ran into the field. Energy pulses were flying left and right. Neons and Temulus were dying all around me. The ground was shaking like a terrible earthquake. There was a loud ringing in my ears as stone walls crash landed all around me. The Kingdom was falling; the Temulus were destroying everything in its path.

A Temulus began to charge at me and within seconds was obliterated by a Neon in its path. I stumbled towards an opening where I could see a reservoir. My energy felt intense, almost as if it wanted to be released, or perhaps something was drawing it out. I wanted to fight. I wanted to find Ford and Creed and join the fight. My energy was through the roof. I could feel pulses running through my veins and coursing through every inch of my body. My focus was on Creed and Ford and finding them to help them defeat the Temulus. My emotions were raging and I couldn't control my anger. My desire. I was trying to feel desire, but I didn't have any incoming thoughts. I thought about Ford, but I felt nothing. What was happening? I thought about his kisses, I thought about him touching me, but nothing fueled my desire.

In that instant I heard a voice inside my head.

"Pen, sweetheart, I can hear your heart beating."

It was Chez.

The ringing in my ears began to heighten and brought me to my knees. I could still hear Chez' voice. "Pen, please don't fight it. I don't want to hurt you."

"Get out of my head!" I screamed. I grabbed my ears to stop the ringing and crumbled into a ball. As I lay in the dirt I could see a body approaching me. It was Ford.

"Penelope! Are you okay? Are you alright? It's me!"

I looked up and as I was about to respond a loud swoosh and gust of wind threw me several feet away from Ford.

It was Chez, and he was on Creed.

"Creed!" I yelled. But he couldn't hear me. His head turned to look at me but his eyes were lost. They were engulfed in red energy. A flash of red drew over my body. Chez stood down from Creed and hovered over Ford and me.

"Give me Pen!," Chez ordered.

Ford stood up and drew his hands in front of him with a green charge. He sent a burst lunging in Chez' direction. Chez blocked it with his red surge and sent Ford to the ground.

"You do know we won the war last time we were here, Ford. What makes you think this time will be any different?" Chez chuckled. "Give me the girl and I won't have to kill any more of your kind. And I won't have to kill this precious creature under my spell." He stroked Creed.

"Ford! No! Don't let him!" I cried.

Ford ran towards Chez again and they began to fight. Pulses of red and green flew all around me.

I ran over to Creed and tried to connect with him. His red eyes glared at me as if he didn't know who I was. Creed squawked loudly and grabbed me with his enormous talons and threw me several feet in the air.

"Penelope! No!" I could hear Chez.

Chez immediately darted towards me and caught me from my fall. "Pen" He looked at me. In that moment, my energy could sense him. I could feel rage and fire.

"Chez, PUT HER DOWN." Ford ordered him.

"Ford, why is this so difficult for you? Why her? You knew what I wanted when I came here. She needs to know." Chez responded with a sly smile.

"Chez! Let me go!" I fought him with all my might.

Ford began to pulse his green energy. "Chez, LET HER GO! I will obliterate you and everything you have." He growled.

"Ford, don't!" I yelled. I wasn't sure where this was coming from. Something was telling me that he couldn't do this, that he couldn't kill Chez."

"Penelope, what are you doing?" Ford breathed heavily with rage.

Chez whispered in my ear. "Stay with me, beautiful. I can take care of you. You can come with me and you can be with Creed. I know you and him are connected."

A tear rolled down my eye. I could hear Ford in my mind.

"Penelope, what are you doing? Don't do this to me."

"Ford, I'm sorry." I cried profusely. "Ford, please just let me go." I couldn't bear to think of Chez killing any more Neons and taking ownership of Creed. This was all because of me. All this destruction, death, depression. I didn't want it anymore. I didn't want to be the cause of any of this.

"You see, Ford. She wants to come with me. She craves to know what she can truly become. Something you can never give her." Chez smiled.

Ford dropped to his knees and his green energy subsided. "Penelope, please."

I looked at Ford and shook my head. "I can't." My voice shook.

"NO!" He let out a piercing yell and shot his electric pulse towards Creed. I cried out in horror as I saw Creed shoot back with force, and then fall to the ground. Chez roared and let me go. I ran over to Creed sobbing and wanting to save him.

"Creed, please, look at me." As I looked into his eyes, his red energy dissipated leaving the weight of his head on my chest.

My mind filled with so many thoughts. My heart was full with sadness, then rage, then hate. I looked over at Ford and my hands began to glow. Only this time, they were red.

"Yes, Pen. This is exactly what's supposed to happen, baby." Chez walked over to me. "Can you feel his rage? He can't control it. It's obvious, or he wouldn't have killed Creed. Your precious, precious companion."

I looked again at Creed and began to yell.

I pointed my hand towards Ford and shot a pulse of red energy. It threw him forcefully against the ground.

"Penelope." He gasped for air. "Please, I won't fight you. I never will."

"You killed Creed!" I yelled.

"Penelope. Control yourself." Ford pleaded.

I could see the red all around me. I turned to look at Chez. He extended his hand. "Pen, come with me."

I looked back at Ford in dismay. I had been betrayed. How could he have killed Creed? To save me? That wasn't the only way. I stared at him on the ground.

"Don't ever come near me," I warned him. "How could you?"

"Penelope. Please." He begged. "Don't go with Chez."

I retracted my red energy pulse and turned to look at Chez. "Get your people out of here. I will go with you." I spoke deliberately.

"Done." He confirmed.

Within minutes, the Temulus had retreated, and all that was left was dust and dead bodies.

Chez took my hand and a force field encircled us. I took one last look at Ford but my anger wouldn't leave me and I couldn't feel anything else.

We departed the Kingdom and were teleported away from the Neon world. I couldn't think about anything but Creed. How could Ford have done this?

I had no idea where I was going, but I knew I had to avenge Creed's death and find Reya. I needed to protect myself, without Ford.

****

I woke up with a feverish headache. God what happened to me? I sat up and could feel the red silk sheets I held before. Oh no. All my memories came flooding back to me in an instant rage. I squinted from the pain in my head. How long had I been out? A wave of anger and sadness came over me as I remembered Ford striking Creed to the ground. A pinch in my heart took over and I felt as if I was about to cry, instead, I pushed the thoughts to the back of my mind.

Sitting up, I could see a light coming from the dark red, velvet curtains that were framed around a 15-foot window and stretched down from a massive ceiling. Curtains that I didn't want to open, a place where I didn't want to be, but I also didn't feel like I could be anywhere else. As I scanned the room, I could see the chair that had once held a red silk dress with a red suit in its place. Written on an envelope sitting atop the suit read, "Put Me On."

I had willingly gone with Chez. It was the only way I could stop the Temulus from bringing The Kingdom down. I wanted to go because Chez was going to take Creed and I couldn't let him do that without taking me as well. Now that Creed was dead I wasn't sure why I was here. My heart hurt trying to resolve why Ford would strike and kill him. He knew I loved Creed and knew him and I were connected. I couldn't comprehend it and now I would never know because I never wanted to see Ford again. Too many thoughts were flooding me and too many emotions for me to think logically. If there was one thing I knew I had to do, it was to find Reya. Creed spent most of his life trying to find her again and I wasn't going to let him down.

He deserved my allegiance, all my love, and fulfillment of my promise to bring Reya home.

Lightning Source UK Ltd.
Milton Keynes UK
UKHW020432031121
393296UK00011B/849

9 780578 742458